R

To help a sick friend, Natalie had offered to hold the fort at her marriage bureau—a kind gesture that had unexpected, and unfortunate, repercussions, when the first person she met there was Miles Denton, furiously angry, and did she but know it, destined to change her whole life—for better or worse!

Books you will enjoy
by ROBERTA LEIGH

FACTS OF LOVE

At twenty-seven, Paula Grayson had been more or less forced into being a newspaper tycoon, but she was still a woman at heart, with all a woman's needs. And all her worldly success did not make up for the heartbreak of knowing that Gregory Scott had been using her to further his own interests . . .

THE SAVAGE ARISTOCRAT

A business trip to Peru ended with Vanessa being kept virtually a prisoner by the autocratic Señor Ramon de la Rivas. But it was an imprisonment that led to her falling in love with him—and that was where her problems really started. For even though she sometimes thought he returned her feelings, he was already pledged to marry another woman . . .

NIGHT OF LOVE

The rich young Greek Leon Panos wanted to marry Alex, but she didn't feel strongly enough about him to accept his proposal—but Leon's tyrannical cousin Nicolas didn't know that, and he set firmly about breaking up the romance. All of which was to lead Alex into far deeper waters with Nicolas than either of them had foreseen . . .

CINDERELLA IN MINK

Nicola Rosten was used to the flattery and deference accorded to a very wealthy woman. Yet Barnaby Grayson mistook her for a down-and-out and set her to work in the kitchen. Should she tell him the truth? How would he react?

RENT A WIFE

BY
ROBERTA LEIGH

MILLS & BOON LIMITED
LONDON W1

All the characters in this book have no existence outside the imagination of the Author, and have no relation whatsoever to anyone bearing the same name or names. They are not even distantly inspired by any individual known or unknown to the Author, and all the incidents are pure invention.

The text of this publication or any part thereof may not be reproduced or transmitted in any form or by any means, electronic or mechanical, including photocopying, recording, storage in an information retrieval system, or otherwise, without the written permission of the publisher.

This book is sold subject to the condition that it shall not by way of trade or otherwise, be lent, resold, hired out or otherwise circulated without the prior consent of the publisher in any form of binding or cover other than that in which it is published and without a similar condition including this condition being imposed on the subsequent purchaser.

First published 1980
Australian copyright 1980
Philippine copyright 1980
This edition 1980

© Roberta Leigh 1980

ISBN 0 263 73308 4

Set in Linotype Baskerville 10 on 11½ pt.

Made and printed in Great Britain by
Richard Clay (The Chaucer Press), Ltd., Bungay, Suffolk

CHAPTER ONE

HALFWAY down Bond Street Natalie Baker paused to admire a window filled with elegant dresses, and a number of passing men paused to admire the admirer.

She was a beautiful creature; taller than average, with russet-coloured hair waving down to her shoulders, and a softly rounded figure with a narrow waist and full breasts. An onlooker might be forgiven for thinking her an actress or model, and even her closest friends were occasionally surprised when they remembered she was a nursery school teacher.

With a half sigh Natalie walked past the window. The expensive apparel displayed were as far out of her reach as the stars. She did not pause until she had gone a further twenty yards and was directly alongside a small plaque fixed to the side of a wall, bearing the words Whitney Marriage Bureau, 2nd Floor. Imagining how pleased her friend Maggie Whitney would be to see her, Natalie climbed the stairs and entered a small waiting room, empty except for a row of chairs and a table displaying a copy of *The Lady* and some out-of-date sewing magazines which, she surmised humorously, symptomised the bulk of Maggie's clients.

Briskly she knocked on the door of the inner office and a Scottish voice bade her come in. Natalie did so, grinning as she saw the amazement on her friend's face.

'Good lord!' Maggie exclaimed. 'I'd no idea you were up in this neck of the woods.'

'I'm a Kensington bird now,' Natalie reminded her. 'And on summer holiday too.'

'How did the move go?' Maggie asked. 'I'm dying to see your apartment.'

'The move went very well,' Natalie smiled, 'and you'll be seeing my nest on Friday. You haven't forgotten you're coming to dinner?'

'Of course not. But I thought I'd come over afterwards.' An odd expression crossed Maggie's homely face. 'I've been getting fearful indigestion lately and I'm careful what I eat.'

'Tell me what you would like and I'll make it for you.'

'At the moment I don't seem to like anything. Even the thought of food nauseates me.'

Natalie looked at her friend more closely and was perturbed by the yellowish tinge of her skin.

'Have you seen a doctor?' she asked.

'I haven't had time. But if I'm not better by the end of the week, I'll pop in to see him on Saturday. But enough about me. Tell me *your* news.'

'I've got none. I have two months' holiday ahead of me and I'm thinking of taking a temporary job. Moving cost me more than I expected and I could do with some cash.'

Natalie perched on the chair and pushed her hair away from her vivid face. The sunlight filtered upon her from the window, but even the bright light could not find a flaw in the creamy skin, and merely emphasised the unusual greeny gold shade of her provocative, slanting eyes.

'You're crazy to go on working for Mrs Hall,' Maggie said crossly. 'If you opened your own nursery school you'd be making a whacking profit for yourself instead of for somebody else.'

'Mrs Hall doesn't make a whacking profit,' Natalie smiled.

'Well, she should, considering the pittance she pays you for looking after all those children. You should go to your bank manager and borrow the money to start upon your own. In six months' time, I might even be able to lend it to you myself.'

'Oh yes?' Natalie looked innocently towards the empty waiting room. 'I don't see clients falling over themselves outside.'

'I don't have the sort of business where clients fall over themselves to get here,' Maggie said dryly. 'But things have been looking up lately and——'

She stopped as the door opened, and Natalie turned quickly, ready to make herself scarce, until she saw it was Maggie's brother. He was fair-haired and of average height, with blue eyes set a shade too closely together, giving him a faintly foxy look. Natalie wondered if she judged Roland too harshly, but she had always found something unlikeable about him. It was partly because she had always thought it unfair of Fate to have given him looks and charm instead of his sister, who would have found them so much more useful.

'Hello, Roland,' she said flatly. 'I thought you were in Australia.'

'I came back a month ago.' He sauntered over to the window and leaned against the side of it. 'You look as gorgeous as ever. Still wasting your time with the toddlers?'

'It's better than wasting it in front of a camera.'

This was said to remind him of the last occasion they had met—before he had emigrated to try his luck in another country—when he had tried to persuade her to pose for some highly lucrative but nude photographs which a friend of his had wanted to take of her.

'I still think you were a fool to turn down the offer,' he said. 'These days, who cares about seeing nude women?'

'A lot of people,' Natalie said promptly, 'otherwise you wouldn't have offered me such a price to pose for your friend!'

He shrugged, as if to show it was all forgotten, and glanced at his wrist watch. It was an elegant gold affair and Natalie wondered if he had done well for himself in Australia. Yet he surely hadn't returned home so soon for a holiday, and if he had come back permanently, why hadn't Maggie said anything to her when they had spoken on the telephone last week?

'Sorry I can't invite you out for lunch, Natalie,' Roland said, moving to the door, 'but I have a date.'

'I'll struggle to live without you,' Natalie rejoined, and managed to give a smile, though it did not reach her eyes. As the door closed behind him she faced her friend. 'Why did Roland come back? I thought he'd emigrated.'

'He did, but he didn't like it there. I'd no idea he was coming home. He just walked in on me.'

'What's he doing now?'

'Helping me, at the moment.' Maggie coloured as she noticed Natalie's beautifully shaped eyebrows raise themselves quizzically. 'I wish you didn't dislike Roland so much.'

'So do I. But I can't help it. He takes advantage of you, Maggie, and it gets my back up.'

'Well, he isn't taking advantage of me at the moment,' his sister said stoutly. 'When I've been too ill to come in he's been running the business single-handed.'

'Too ill to come in?' Natalie was shocked. 'I thought you said you were just a bit off colour?'

'Some days have been worse than others,' Maggie admitted, looking sorry she had given so much away. 'I can cope with the indigestion, but the nausea gets me down.'

'If you don't promise to see the doctor right away,' Natalie exploded, 'I'll drag you there myself.'

'Don't fuss!' said Maggie. 'I told you I'll see one over the weekend. Anyway, it's been good for Roland to run the office on his own from time to time. To begin with he only did it to help out, but now I think he's becoming interested in it for its own sake. He's awfully good with the women clients.'

'I'll bet he is,' Natalie said.

It was Roland's ability to charm the female sex that had so often led to his downfall in the past. If she remembered rightly, it was a particularly torrid affair with a married woman which had prompted him to leave England so hurriedly. But now he was back and obviously trying to inveigle himself into his sister's business.

'I think you'd be very unwise to let Roland work here permanently,' she said bluntly.

'I'll eventually need someone to help me,' Maggie told her. 'And I'd rather have someone I know, than a stranger. *You* haven't changed your mind, have you?'

' 'Fraid not.' Natalie was regretful. 'This sort of occupation isn't my scene. I love working with young children and I'd be unhappy doing anything else. I know it's old-fashioned of me, but I can't help it.'

'It isn't old-fashioned,' Maggie declared stoutly. 'But

coming from you, it's unexpected. A girl with your looks should be doing something glamorous and exciting.'

'Don't judge the fruit by the skin,' Natalie grinned. 'I may look as exotic as a passion fruit, but inside I'm a homely apple!'

'A Golden Delicious!' Maggie grinned back. 'Never a Granny Smith!'

Natalie flushed and stood up.

'Is it still on for Friday, then? If you feel too off colour to make it, let's opt for another night.'

'No, Friday will be fine. But no big meal, please. I'm only coming to see your new apartment. If I'm a bit late, it'll be because I've stopped in on the way to see the doctor.'

In the event, Maggie did not come at all. She was taken violently ill with stomach pains as she was preparing to leave the office on Friday, and Roland took her in a taxi to the emergency department of the Middlesex Hospital.

'They think it's her gall bladder,' Roland said, when he telephoned Natalie to let her know why Maggie had not turned up. 'They've kept her in and they're going to do some tests. She said if you're free at any time during the weekend, she would love to see you.'

'I'll go tomorrow,' Natalie promised, knowing she would not be easy in her mind until she had seen her friend for herself. Disliking Roland as much as she did, she was reluctant to believe anything he said.

Promptly at three the next afternoon, she was sitting beside Maggie in a large hospital ward. She was careful to hide her dismay at the sight of the haggard face on the pillow in front of her. Maggie looked desperately ill and there was a dullness in her eyes that spoke of drugs to combat the pain.

'It's definitely my gall bladder,' she explained, after she had thanked Natalie for the selection of magazines she had brought. 'Angus says I'll have to have it out.'

'Angus? Don't tell me you're already on first names with your surgeon?'

'He isn't my surgeon. He's a Registrar here and I knew him years ago in Aberdeen.'

'You Scots get everywhere,' Natalie smiled.

'That's certainly true of Angus. He's been all over the world since he qualified—that's why we lost touch with each other. I had no idea he was back in England or attached to this hospital.'

'So every cloud has a silver lining!'

Maggie's plain face looked unexpectedly pretty as colour suffused it, and Natalie wondered if Angus could be a romantic part of her friend's past. She had always been extraordinarily shy with men and it was this that had prompted her to start the Marriage Bureau. She was convinced there were other people like herself who were too shy to find members of the opposite sex without someone else's help.

'And how long does this Angus of yours expect you to be in hospital?' Natalie asked.

'About two or three weeks. That's why I'm so glad you've come to see me. I hate to ask you this, but——'

'The answer is yes,' Natalie interrupted, 'and don't be so silly. Of course I'll help you.'

The look of relief on Maggie's face was sufficient compensation for Natalie. The prospect of spending her two months' holiday taking care of the Whitney Marriage Bureau was distinctly dampening. But since the alternative was to allow Roland to run it on his own, she had no choice. She might not be the greatest business woman, but she was at least honest.

'You won't mind Roland helping you?' Maggie asked pleadingly. 'It's important for him to have something to do. He's written off to various people who have promised to help him find a job, but he's still waiting to hear.'

'Don't worry about Roland. We'll manage to survive without killing each other.'

Natalie opened her bag and searched for some paper and a pen. 'I'm sure there are things I need to know about the office, so if you could put me in the picture....'

'There isn't all that much to know. The main thing is to remember that everyone must pay their introductory fee and that you can't introduce one person to another unless they're *both* on your books. If you don't follow that rule, you can lose your licence.'

'I don't see how I can introduce someone to anybody who *isn't* on the books,' Natalie grinned.

'What I mean is that you mustn't start introducing people to your friends.'

'Why not?' Natalie asked pertly. 'So long as I make my friends pay their introductory fee.'

Maggie laughed. 'I know we need some more clients, but I don't want to get them that way.'

'How *does* one get them?'

'By advertising—which I can't afford to do properly—and by recommendation, which is what I rely on at the moment. I'm sure you'll do splendidly,' Maggie went on thoughtfully. 'It might even encourage you to think in terms of marriage for yourself.'

'I think of marriage the whole time,' Natalie said

promptly. 'The trouble is I can't find a male to fit my requirements!'

'Maybe you require too much.'

'I don't intend to lower my sights yet awhile,' Natalie said firmly. 'Not until I'm on the wrong side of thirty.'

'You'll be married long before then,' Maggie assured her. 'Gosh, if I were as beautiful as you....'

'You have a beautiful character, Maggie. That's much more lasting than a beautiful face.'

Maggie suddenly leaned back against the pillows, looking pale and tired, and Natalie quickly said her goodbyes and left the ward.

Outside the hospital she realised she had forgotten to ask Maggie exactly what Roland did at the office, and decided that no matter what he had done when his sister was in charge, she herself was going to curtail his activities. One thing he was not going to do was to have his fingers on any money. Maggie might genuinely believe her brother had changed for the better in the past year, but Natalie did not believe a leopard could change its spots. They might fade or appear less noticeable in a different light, but they would always be there.

At nine o'clock on Monday morning Natalie unlocked the door of the Whitney Marriage Bureau with more than a little trepidation. It was one thing to help her friend out—which she had occasionally done—but quite another to be left in sole charge. But it was too late to back out. By now, Maggie was on her way to the operating theatre, content in the knowledge that her business was in capable hands.

'It had better be,' Natalie muttered aloud, knowing how hard her friend had struggled to make a success of this venture.

But it was not until she started to examine the books to see the cash flow position and what the expenses were likely to be each week that she realised how tight the situation still was. The agency had quite a few clients, and in the year it had been operating, a high proportion of successes had been achieved. But the rent of this tiny office was high, and even the minimum advertising which had been done had still left an appreciable dent in the finances. There was certainly no money available to pay Roland the amount he had been drawing each week, and she determined that no more money would go his way unless he earned it.

Picking up the letters that had come in on the second post, Natalie sat at Maggie's desk and opened them. They were mainly circulars and bills, though one was from a client who wished to have her money refunded as she had decided not to continue with any more introductions. Letter in hand, Natalie went over to the filing cabinet to look up the terms of engagement, and found that if a certain number of introductions had already been arranged, then the fees were not returnable.

Carefully she composed a reply, being regretful but firm and suggesting that since the agency was legally within its rights in not returning any fee, the client might wish to reconsider her decision and use up the requisite number of introductions.

She was signing the letter when Roland walked in, and his warm smile added to the discomfiture she felt at not liking him.

'Maggie told me you'd agreed to come in full time and hold the fort,' he said, perching on the front of her desk. 'I would have done so myself if you hadn't volunteered, but I think you'll handle the men much better than I would.'

'Women are much more in your line,' Natalie agreed, and felt his light blue eyes rest speculatively on her.

But he decided to ignore any hidden meaning behind her remark, and sliding off the desk he sauntered to the door.

'I've got some personal business to attend to this morning,' he said casually, 'but I'll be back in time for you to go to lunch.'

'I intended to close the office during the lunch hour,' Natalie said.

Roland shook his head. 'Maggie doesn't. She says you often get clients coming in between one and two.'

Natalie nodded without actually stating whether or not she was going to do as he said, knowing that in this way, if she wished to change her mind she could do so.

'Be seeing you,' he said with a wave, and sauntered out.

Natalie stared after him. Whatever it was that Roland did to help his sister, his hours here were obviously limited, which made her feel considerably less guilty at her decision to cut down on the money he was drawing.

The telephone rang and with a quickened heartbeat she answered it. It was a wrong number and she put back the receiver and looked around morosely. No one could say the joint was jumping! Tomorrow she would bring in a book to read.

At lunchtime Roland telephoned to say that one of his appointments was taking longer than he had expected and he doubted if he would be back in time to stand in for her during the lunch break. Assuring him she could manage on her own, Natalie immediately hurried down the two flights of stairs to the street and into a nearby coffee shop. Ten minutes later she was back in the office with a mug of coffee and a healthy supply of chicken sandwiches.

Refreshed by the food and the breath of fresh air, she worked quietly until almost four o'clock, looking through the files and seeing who had met whom and when, as well as how many more introductions still needed to be made. She was debating whether to make herself a cup of tea—there was only powdered milk, but it was better than nothing—when she heard the door of the outer office open and quick, firm steps cross the floor.

She waited for a knock, but the door of her office was pushed forward with a sharpness which rustled the papers of her desk as a tall, fiercely angry man strode forward and stopped abruptly at the edge of her desk.

Even though he said nothing, the fury that emanated from him was almost tangible. It was visible in the taut line of his jaw, thrust belligerently forward, and it blazed from stormy eyes that were almost the colour of sherry. He was tall, but bone-thin, which made him seem even taller as he leaned menacingly forward.

'You don't look criminally negligent—I'll say that for you,' he said in a soft voice made all the more frightening because it was obviously under the most tight control. 'Yet you are, without doubt, the most irresponsible person I have ever had the misfortune to encounter. How you got your licence is beyond me, but I assure you it won't be in your possession for much longer!'

The words ceased abruptly, as if the momentum of

his anger had left him spent, and Natalie spoke into the silence, surprised to hear her voice so calm.

'You obviously expect a coherent reply to your outburst, but since I don't happen to know what you're talking about, I'm afraid I can't give you one, Mr—er——'

'Denton,' he snapped. 'Miles Denton, and I'm talking about my sister.'

Natalie's blank look made the man's face tighten with temper again.

'I wouldn't have thought you had so many clients that you can't remember any particular one of them,' he added sarcastically.

'I'm afraid——'

'You've every right to be afraid,' he cut in ruthlessly. 'By the time I've finished with you, you'll never be able to open shop again in London. And don't think you'll be able to set up this racket of yours anywhere else either!'

'It would be a help if you told me what we're supposed to have done, that you consider so reprehensible.'

'Don't you know?' he almost shouted the words. 'You take my sister on your books—a girl so young and pretty that no reputable agency would even dream of accepting her—and you then introduce her to an absolute scoundrel!'

'A scoundrel?' Natalie questioned.

'Unless you think it normal behaviour for a man to get an introduction to a girl and then let her pay for him when he takes her out and accepts lavish presents into the bargain. If that's what you call vetting everyone on your books,' he added, extracting a copy of the agency terms and conditions from his pocket and slamming it down on the desk, 'then you might as well tear this up and throw it in the dustbin!'

Natalie began to understand the reason for the man's anger. Yet she was still not completely in the picture.

'Are you saying our agency introduced your sister to this man?'

'You catch on quickly.'

'More quickly than your sister,' Natalie snapped, angered by his rudeness. 'If Miss Denton came here seeking introductions that might lead to marriage, then——'

'At eighteen?' he stormed. 'A blonde bombshell of eighteen needing to have her boy-friends found for her? If you'd had any integrity at all, you'd have sent her packing.'

Since this was precisely what Natalie would have done, she was at a loss what to say. How could Maggie have taken the girl and, even more alarming, who was the scoundrel? Yet she dared not show her thoughts.

'As far as British law is concerned,' she said aloud, 'if your sister is over eighteen she is able to make her own decisions. Also, if your sister had had no difficulty meeting a man she wouldn't have come here.'

The sherry gold eyes darkened with fury and Natalie stiffened in her chair, afraid that the man might lunge forward and hit her.

But with an effort he calmed down, though his eyes still glittered and his mouth was a narrow line.

'No one with intelligence would have taken Gillian as a client, and no agency of integrity would have accepted a man like Rodney White.'

'R-Rodney White?' Natalie stammered, a dreadful suspicion coming into her mind.

'Don't tell me you don't remember him either!' came the sarcastic comment, as the man looked round the sparsely furnished office.

'I was merely repeating the name to make sure I'd heard it correctly,' Natalie said hastily.

'I have never been accused of speaking with less than perfect diction,' came the cold reply. 'And I hope that what I am about to say now will also be perfectly clear. I consider your agency a sham and a disgrace, and I intend to put you out of business.'

He turned his head again, as if looking for a chair, then decided against it and went to stand by the window. The light coming from behind him emphasised his leanness and his pale complexion. It was not the pallor of ill-health; he merely looked as if he spent no time in the sun, which was surprising, for it was mid-August and the weather had been perfect for weeks. Natalie wondered anxiously if he had just come out of prison, or if he was a mental patient who had escaped from detention.

'Perhaps you'd like to tell me exactly what happened to your sister,' she said soothingly. 'I can assure you all our clients are extremely satisfied with us and we have never yet had a complaint from anyone.'

'Well, you've got one now,' he said rudely, 'and it will put you out of business.' His voice hardened. 'Don't you make enquiries about people before you accept them as clients, or are you so hard up for them that you'll take anyone who has money to waste?'

'None of our clients waste their money,' Natalie said sharply, 'and every one we take is personally vetted.'

'Then how did White get through? Or is he an ex-boy-friend of *yours*?'

'That remark is quite uncalled-for!' Natalie's voice shook with anger. 'Though we vet our clients, Mr Denton, we don't have the Secret Service do a run-down on them. Nor do we act as watchdog when two of our clients are introduced to each other. If your sister went Dutch treat with Mr White or gave him presents of which you disapprove, I suggest you discuss it with her rather than with us.'

'It isn't the giving of presents that I dislike,' the man replied, 'but the fact that the scoundrel took them and then a day later tried to sell them. If you consider Rodney White a man suitable for marriage, then I'd like to meet the man considered unsuitable!'

The suspicion Natalie had felt on first hearing the name Rodney White now became a firm possibility.

'Are you sure your sister met this—er—this young man here?'

'Yes. The introduction came from you—and it's the last one you'll be giving. That's what I came to tell you.'

He swung round to the door and Natalie jumped to her feet.

'Mr Denton,' she called, 'what are you going to do?'

'Make sure your licence is taken away.'

'You can't do that!'

'Try to stop me!'

He flung open the door and banged it behind him. The sound of crashing footsteps reverberated in Natalie's ears as she rushed across the room, but even as she reached the stairs, she saw the tall thin figure disappearing through the entrance.

Slowly she returned to the office. Rodney White and Roland Whitney—it was too much of a coincidence to be one, and all her fears about Maggie's brother surfaced again. From the moment he had reappeared the other day she had known he was up to no good. What she did not know was why Maggie had introduced him to one of her clients when she had emphasised that one must never introduce one's personal friends or relatives to anyone on the agency books. Shaking her head in bewilderment, Natalie paced the floor.

If Mr Denton carried out his threat, it would be disastrous for Maggie, and at the moment she could not think of any way of stopping him.

CHAPTER TWO

NATALIE was still pacing the floor when Roland strolled in. He had the air of a man well lunched and well satisfied with himself, which did nothing whatever to endear him to Natalie.

'Hello,' he said pleasantly. 'Had a good day?'

'No.'

'A quiet one, I take it?'

'No.'

His eyebrows rose at the terseness of her replies and he went over to the desk, glanced at a couple of letters, and then put them down again.

'Can I help you?' Natalie asked quietly.

'Isn't that *my* question?' he said.

'The agency can manage very well without your help, Roland.'

'You're making that pretty clear. But then you've always made your opinion of me clear, haven't you?'

'It doesn't seem to worry you,' Natalie said shortly.

'Why should it? You're not the only fish in the sea.'

'That's for sure. And there's one particular little fish I want to talk about.' She paused. 'It's called Denton.'

Any doubts Natalie might have had disappeared as she saw the shifty look in Roland's eyes.

'I'm not going to ask if you know her,' she went on, 'since you obviously do.'

'That's right.'

'Was it also right to take presents from her and then sell them?'

'She knows?' Roland looked startled and then turned an unbecoming red.

'Her brother knows,' Natalie replied, 'which amounts to the same thing.'

'It was my birthday,' he said suddenly. 'And it was only a small gift.'

'It can still cost Maggie her business. She has no business to introduce you to a client.'

'She didn't introduce me.'

The words were quiet, but loud enough for Natalie to hear them, though it took her a moment to realise what they meant.

'So you introduced yourself?' she said. 'Are you so short of girl-friends that you had to go through the agency files?'

'Of course not. But she happened to be particularly pretty.'

'And she came to a marriage bureau to meet a young man?' Natalie said disbelievingly.

'Lots of young girls come here,' Roland shrugged. 'Don't run away with the idea that marriage bureaus are only for divorcees or spinsters or misfits. There are lots of young people who find it difficult to meet others of their own age.'

'Spare me the run-down on the type of clients we can expect,' she said coldly, 'and tell me how you came to meet Miss Denton.'

He hesitated, then knowing she was not going to be put off, he gave a lift of his shoulders. 'I was in the other office when I saw her come in. I liked the look of her and it seemed a good idea to give her a call.'

'And pretend you'd been given her number by the Bureau?'

'Too true.'

'Don't you know we're not allowed to do that?' Natalie blazed at him. 'It's illegal to introduce a client to someone who isn't on your books.'

'Oh, have a heart!' Roland protested. 'Who's going to know?'

'Her brother. He was here an hour ago, mad as a bull with corns.'

Roland looked disquieted. 'Bad luck still seems to be following me around.'

'Not bad luck, Roland—bad management. If you wanted to get money out of a girl you should have played your games further away from home.'

'Okay, I made a mistake. I promise it won't happen again.'

'You're right on that one,' she said calmly, 'because Mr Denton is going to get Maggie's licence revoked.'

She knew a momentary pleasure as she saw the colour ebb from Roland's face.

'He wouldn't be such a swine!'

'He thinks *you* are the swine.'

'But he can't blame the agency for what I did!'

'Unfortunately he does. You see, he happens to believe we introduced you to his sister.'

'Why didn't you tell him that Maggie knew nothing about it?'

'Because it wasn't until he left that I began to work it out and realised what had happened.' She waved a hand at him. 'And you confirmed it.'

Moodily Roland kicked at the carpet. 'What are you going to do?'

'I don't know.' She gave him a look of contempt. How typical of Roland that question was! Not 'what can I do to put things right?' but 'what are *you* going to do?'

Of course she had to do something. Much as she despised Roland she could not stand by and see Maggie's business collapse. She glanced at her watch. It was five o'clock. Too late for Mr Denton—no matter how high his temper—to report them to the Westminster Council today. The earliest he could do so would be tomorrow at ten. By then, with any luck, she might be able to change his mind.

'I'll have to go and see him,' she said, and then muttered angrily: 'Except that I don't know where he lives and there are probably hundreds of Dentons in the directory.'

'His first name is Miles,' Roland informed her. 'Gilly told me. Miles Edward, and he's a doctor.'

Reaching for the directory, Natalie scanned through the Dentons. There was only one with Miles E. in front of it and that was at an address in Harley Street, where Mr Miles E. Denton had both his home and his consulting rooms. The initials after his name told her he was a surgeon, and a highly qualified one too. She jotted down the address and put it into her handbag.

'I'm going to see him right away,' she announced.

'Would you like me to drive you there?' Roland asked. 'My car is parked round the corner.'

'You keep as far away from Mr Denton as possible,' she snapped. 'The last thing I want is for him to see me with you.'

She locked the door of the office, then pushed past Roland and ran down the stairs.

'Don't bother coming in tomorrow,' she called up to him. 'If I need anyone to help me out, I'll ring the Snake House at the Zoo!'

She was still angry as her taxi drove slowly up Harley Street, but it was an anger directed against Roland rather than at the man she was on her way to see. Indeed, she now found she had a sneaking sympathy for Miles Denton, though she still considered he had behaved like a boor when he had come round to see her.

It was not until she was facing the highly polished front door, with its distinguished brass plate bearing the name M. E. Denton, that she had her first doubts at coming here. Perhaps she should have telephoned first. But if he had refused to see her, it would have made it impossible for her to call on him. Firmly she pressed the bell, then clasped her fingers round her handbag and held it in front of her defensively. The door opened and a pleasant-faced middle-aged woman asked her name.

'I would like to see Mr Denton.'

'Miss Baker?' the woman repeated, and gave a slight frown. 'I'm afraid your name isn't on Mr Denton's list of appointments.'

'I don't have an appointment.'

'Mr Denton never sees anyone without an———'

'I haven't come to see Mr Denton professionally,' Natalie interposed.

'Oh.' The woman went slightly pink. 'I hadn't realised it was personal. I'll go and tell Mr Denton you're here.'

Realising he wouldn't know her name, Natalie said swiftly: 'Please tell him it's the young woman he saw at the agency earlier today.'

Struggling to hide her curiosity, and not succeeding very well, the receptionist ushered Natalie into a large waiting room that faced on to Harley Street, and told her to wait.

Alone, Natalie looked around her. Unlike most rooms of this kind, it was beautifully furnished and did not look as if it had been put together with throw-outs. It had the appearance of a normal sitting-room, with an antique Persian carpet on the floor, well-upholstered settees in rose damask, and a large round centre table which was highly polished and obviously valuable. Its top was covered with magazines, and she picked one up, then put it down again, too nervous to read.

Walking over to the large mirror above the mantelpiece, she tried to see herself in it. But the light was dim and her face peered back at her indistinctly, though her hair glowed russet gold, the colour of maple leaves in autumn.

'Mr Denton will see you now.'

Natalie swung round with a start, then hastily followed the receptionist into the hall and down a long corridor lined with exceptionally good watercolours at eye level, and an equally good Chinese runner underfoot. Mr Denton might be short on manners, she thought scornfully, but he was well endowed with worldly goods.

At the end of the corridor the woman stopped and turned the handle of a leather-faced door, then motioned Natalie to step through.

Hiding her nervousness, Natalie did so. A few yards in front of her, seated behind a massive Regency desk, sat the man she had come to see. He half rose, then seated himself again as the door closed and they were alone.

'I won't keep you a moment,' he said without expression, and bent over some papers. There was the sound of a pen scratching, then it was set down with a single precise movement and cold sherry-coloured eyes stared at her.

'It won't do any good to come and plead with me,

Miss——' He glanced at a pad in front of him and then quickly up at her. 'Miss Baker. My mind is made up about what I intend to do.'

'If you're the sort of man who never changes his mind when events change, Mr Denton, I'm sorry for your patients!'

Colour tinged his face, but he said nothing, and Natalie knew he was waiting for her to explain herself. It was not easy to do, for if she admitted the real identity of Rodney White, and said what an unsavoury character he was, she would be putting Maggie in a vulnerable position. Though wild horses would not have made her confess her real feelings to the man in front of her, deep in her heart she considered her friend very much to blame for not realising the sort of person her brother was. To have allowed him to work in the office, surrounded by women whose loneliness and need of companionship put them in a particularly vulnerable position, had been foolhardy in the extreme.

'Well, Miss Baker?' Miles Denton said impatiently. 'Please say what you've come here to say and then go. I'm a busy man.'

'No one else is waiting to see you.'

'I've had a busy day,' he said icily. 'I was operating at eight and didn't finish until three, when I then did my rounds of the wards before returning here. In two hours from now I'm due to speak at a medical dinner. I am neither in the mood, nor do I have the wish to listen to any excuses you may have concocted in your defence.'

Temper gave Natalie courage. 'You found the time to come and accuse me unjustly,' she replied, 'so you should at least spare the time to hear my explanation.'

She took a step forward and then stopped, but it

was enough for him to remember his manners, and in silence he pointed to a chair. She perched on the end of it, her bag on her lap, glad that its weight helped to still the trembling of her legs.

'The man whom your sister met,' she began, 'was not a client of the Agency. He—he isn't on our books. He is—he is a relation of Miss Whitney who owns the agency.'

If Miles Denton was surprised, he hid it well.

'What sort of relation?'

'A brother.'

'And you?'

'I'm just a friend who's helping her out. Miss Whitney was taken ill yesterday and had an emergency operation his morning. She won't be available for several weeks.'

'How convenient!'

'You can see her in the Middlesex Hospital if you don't believe me,' Natalie flashed. 'I'm sure it will do wonders for her recovery to know you're planning to take away her livelihood.'

'Spare me the sentiment,' he said coldly. 'If you came here to help Miss Whitney, I'm afraid you've done exactly the opposite. Presumably she knows the sort of man her brother is, and to introduce him to *anyone*—most of all a girl of eighteen—is criminally negligent. She *deserves* to have her business licence taken away.'

'No one will do that without first hearing her side of the story.'

'Really?' I happen to know the chairman of the Westminster Licensing Committee.'

It was a quelling thought, but Natalie refused to be vanquished.

'Maggie—Miss Whitney never introduced Roland to your sister. She would be horrified if she even thought they'd met. But Roland glimpsed your sister when she came in and he—he contacted her. So you see, the agency is not to blame.'

'On the contrary. You are telling me that the agency is so badly run that any Tom, Dick or—Roland can get hold of a client's name.'

'It wasn't like that,' Natalie said desperately. 'Roland was helping out at the Agency because Maggie was feeling ill. She'd be horrified if she knew he'd looked in any of the files and used the information for his personal benefit.'

'Aren't they kept locked?'

'Of course they are. But only at night, not during the day. Maggie never leaves the office and there's no one else there.'

'Except a ne'er-do-well who snooped around and found what he wanted. Miss Whitney should know better than to employ untrustworthy people.'

'She doesn't know her brother is untrustworthy,' Natalie asserted. 'That's the trouble. She merely thinks he's irresponsible. He emigrated to Australia last year and came back a few weeks ago. He hasn't found a job yet, and as she wasn't feeling well, he offered to help her.'

'And to help himself.'

A frightening thought struck Natalie.

'Do you think there were other women besides your sister?' she gasped.

'That's for you to find out,' the man said impatiently. 'But I would be surprised if my sister was the only one. Men of that type like to have several strings to their bow. But my only concern is for Gillian.'

'She didn't come to any harm,' Natalie ventured slowly. 'I mean, she must have—she must have liked Roland to have gone out with him and given him a present. The cufflinks were for his birthday,' she added, hoping this was sufficient excuse, 'so it wasn't so terrible for Roland to have accepted them.'

'We have different standards of what is acceptable, Miss Baker,' the man replied evenly.

'Haven't you ever accepted a birthday present from a woman, Mr Denton?'

'Not to the value of five hundred pounds.'

'*What?*'

His expression grew mocking. 'Yes, Miss Baker, I did say five hundred pounds. The cufflinks were gold and diamond ones.'

'I didn't realise.' Natalie looked down at her hands. 'I—er—of course I'll make sure Roland returns them.'

'How can he when he's already sold them?' Miles Denton stood up. 'But that's all in the past. My concern is for the future. If Miss Whitney doesn't understand the sort of man her brother is, then she's not a good enough judge of character to be in charge of a marriage bureau.'

'She's an excellent judge of character,' Natalie corrected. 'She's been enormously successful since she started. Do you know that forty per cent of the people on her books have already met their partners? That's awfully high, you know.'

'I don't know, nor do I care.'

'But you should care. You should care terribly before you put someone out of business. It's an awful thing to do.' Distress made Natalie's voice break. 'I give you my word of honour that Roland will never see your sister again. I won't let him come back to the

Agency and I'll make sure Maggie knows the truth as soon as she's better. But you mustn't get the Agency closed. It wouldn't be fair!'

Without realising it, she had jumped up and was facing Miles Denton. Her head was tilted back, the better to plead, and she was unaware of the lovely picture she made. Her eyes were luminous with tears and her hair waved gently down each side of her face, its rich colour gaining added lustre from the lamp which shone behind her.

'Please, Mr Denton,' she said huskily, 'Maggie has put every penny she owns into the Agency. If you take away her licence she'll have nothing. You can't be so cruel!'

'Being cruel to your friend might be a kindness to a lot of other women,' came the quiet statement.

'But Roland won't come back,' Natalie repeated. 'I give you my word on that, and I'll give you Maggie's word, too.'

'You can't speak for another person.'

'Then take *my* word,' she pleaded. 'Please, Mr Denton.'

Thoughtfully he rubbed his chin. Now that he was no longer angry it did not have the same belligerent look, though it was still firm, as were the fingers that moved along it. Thin fingers, she noticed, long and with beautifully shaped nails. The hands of a surgeon.

She looked quickly away from him, then as quickly brought her eyes back to his face, determined not to lessen his embarrassment; and she could see that he was embarrassed from the way he nibbled at his lower lip. Surprisingly it was not as thin as she had first imagined. Released from its earlier tautness, it looked fuller and well shaped. His features really were a mass of contradictions, and she suspected that the same could be said of his character.

'You've pleaded excellently for a poor cause, Miss Baker,' he said suddenly. 'But I'm still not convinced I should do as you ask.'

'Of course you should do it,' she said impetuously, and flung out her hand. It touched his arm and he drew back so swiftly that her face flooded with colour. 'I'm sorry,' she said stiffly. 'I wasn't threatening you.'

'I'm not frightened,' he said dryly, and moved to the door. 'I'll think over what you've said, Miss Baker. I won't make any promises, but I shall give you my answer tomorrow.'

'Do you enjoy prolonging the agony?' she asked acidly.

'Of course,' he replied. 'That's why I'm a surgeon.'

She knew she deserved the rebuke but could not bring herself to apologise. Head high, she went to the door.

'I'll wait to hear from you, Mr Denton.'

She was halfway down the corridor when she heard him behind her.

'I must open the door for you,' he said easily. 'My receptionist has already gone.'

Silently she continued to walk until they reached the front door.

As he opened it for her, a taxi stopped almost directly opposite it and a beautiful girl, all long slim legs and sleek blonde hair, emerged from it and raced up the steps.

'Miles darling,' she said in a soft, breathless voice. 'I hope this is your last patient.'

'Not a patient at all,' he said swiftly, bestowing a light kiss on the face held up to him.

Watching the way his expression changed, Natalie could not believe it was the same man, for he looked so much younger and friendlier as he allowed the volubly talking girl to catch hold of his arm and cling to it.

'Then I'm not too early,' she said adoringly. 'I know you said I shouldn't arrive before seven, but I finished my shopping ages ago and I didn't know what to do with myself.'

'You're here now,' he said gently, and extricated himself from her hold. He opened the door wider and looked pointedly at Natalie. 'I'll call you tomorrow,' he said.

Natalie gave him a direct look and went down the steps.

'Why do you have to call her, darling?' she heard the girl ask plaintively. 'Who is she?'

The man's answer was shut off by the closing of the door, and only then did Natalie glance round and look at the house, noticing how beautifully kept it was. The steps were pristine white, as if they had been freshly cleaned, and the single brass plate on the front door signified that only one person had their consulting rooms there. It was Miles Denton's home too, she remembered, and pulled a face at the knowledge that the whole house was his. He must be a highly successful surgeon indeed. What could a man like that know of hardship and the difficulties of running a business with insufficient capital? She thought of Maggie and muttered grimly to herself.

'He can't ruin her. I won't let him!'

They were fine words, and they bolstered her courage for a short while. But by the time she reached her own home she had acknowledged that, in the last resort, there was very little she could do to stop him.

CHAPTER THREE

NATALIE spent the rest of the evening considering ways of persuading Miles Denton—horrible man—to change his mind about trying to revoke the licence of the Marriage Bureau. She toyed with the idea of getting Maggie to telephone him from her sickbed, but was by no means convinced this would have any effect on him. As a surgeon he was used to sick people and would be sufficiently hard-hearted to ignore any pleas, no matter how justifiable. The thought of him increased her anger, and her temper bubbled dangerously near to boiling point.

She was still simmering with rage when she unlocked the door of the office the next morning, almost anticipating that an inspector would be on her doorstep. But all was calm.

She collected the post, changed the flowers on the desk and then sat down and began to go through the post. At ten o'clock Roland arrived, looking as nonchalant as ever.

She glared at him.

'I thought I told you not to come here any more?'

'You did,' he said, 'but this is still my sister's agency, not yours.'

'As long as I'm in charge I want you to stay away.'

He sat down in the hard chair facing the desk, managing by some extraordinary feat to look quite comfortable in it.

'I'm a bit short of the ready since coming back from

Australia,' he announced. 'Hence my offering to help Maggie out.'

'And helping yourself into the bargain, I'll be bound. When Maggie finds out what you did....'

'Are you going to be the one to tell her?' Roland sneered. 'It will hardly help her to make a speedy recovery.'

'I've every intention of telling her as soon as she gets better,' Natalie asserted. 'Did you really believe you wouldn't be found out?'

'Yes, I did. I never thought Gilly would rush off like an idiot and confide in big brother.'

'I don't know that she did,' said Natalie, and was immediately sorry she had spoken, for she saw Roland's interest perk up and knew he was re-assessing the situation. If Gillian Denton had told her brother about him, it would have meant she was furious with Roland. But if she hadn't, there might still be a possibility that she could be used again.

Swallowing the anger which was welling up inside her, Natalie said: 'Don't get any ideas about starting up with Gillian Denton again. If her brother finds out you're still seeing her, he would not only put us out of business, but have you put behind bars for false pretences!'

'I didn't do anything criminal,' Roland said sulkily, his eyes avoiding hers, and she was sure he was not as confident as he tried to pretend. Criminal his action might not have been, but it was sufficiently reprehensible to harm a reputation that was already unsavoury.

'The police have long memories, Roland,' she said. 'If Mr Denton went to see them and complained about you, they might remember a few other things you've done.'

'Don't give me that.' Roland stood up and brushed some dust from his jacket. 'There's no harm in selling a few dud cars, and there's nothing criminal in running off with your boss's wife.' He gave her an insolent smile. 'But the sooner you give me some money the sooner I'll get out of your hair. Fifty pounds will do for the moment.'

'Where do you think I'm going to get that amount? There's only ten pounds in the petty cash.'

'You can write me a cheque, angel. You're a director of Maggie's company, aren't you?'

'That still doesn't give me the right to sign your sister's cheque book,' Natalie said coldly.

'Then I'll have to go to the hospital and ask her to do it instead. She was going to give me some money anyway, but it slipped her mind when she was taken ill.'

Unwilling to have him pester Maggie, and knowing he was quite capable of doing so, Natalie took out her own cheque book and wrote out the amount he had asked for.

'There'll be no more after this,' she said, handing it to him. 'If you can't find a job to suit your ambition, I suggest you become a refuse collector. You've made enough mess of your life to start doing some clearing up!'

'Very funny,' he said sourly.

'Or you could go back to Australia,' she suggested.

'You'd like that, wouldn't you?' He folded the cheque. 'But don't bank on it, angel.' He strolled to the door and closed it quietly behind him.

Resolutely Natalie concentrated on the correspondence and tried to put Roland out of her mind. But she could not help wondering how many other women he had contacted apart from Gillian, and if she would have to deal with any more irate relations.

Luckily for her peace of mind, there were two new clients that morning, one a woman of forty, and the other a divorced man in his fifties who, after thirty years of marriage, was not finding it easy to make friends again.

'When my wife and I split up, our friends were wary of me,' he said. 'The husbands were happy to go on seeing me, but the wives were afraid I might give their menfolk ideas.' He half smiled. 'You know the sort of thing; that I'd tell them how wonderful it was to be single and what fun they were missing.' The half smile disappeared and he looked sad. 'They don't realise I hate every minute of my freedom. The divorce wasn't my idea, you know, but I wasn't given much choice.'

Natalie tried not to let her sympathy affect her judgment as she listened to the man's story and made detailed notes about him.

'It took me a long time to make up my mind to come here,' he confessed as he stood up to leave. 'It seems almost indecent to admit you can't find a partner for yourself and need someone else to do it for you.'

'We're always getting other people to do things for us,' Natalie assured him. 'That's what experts are for. You're not embarrassed to go to a doctor when you're ill, or to a tailor when you need a new suit. Right now you're shopping for a wife, so you sensibly come to a marriage bureau.'

'I never thought of it that way,' the man said in surprise.

'Not many people do.'

'Well, if you can sort me out, I know a few others

like myself, who'd be more than delighted to come here.'

Promising to do her best for him, Natalie closed the door and settled down to eat her sandwich lunch. She would have closed the office and taken a proper break had it not been for the fear that Miles Denton might telephone her. If he rang and she was out, he would probably think she was not worried about what he might do, and he might then conceivably go and do it.

Her anxiety increased and the sandwich she was trying to eat stuck in her throat. She was coughing so hard she did not hear the knock on the door, and it was only when it opened that she looked up and saw the tall, lean man standing there, looking at her with disapproval.

Scarlet-faced, she wiped the crumbs from her mouth. 'Mr Denton,' she mumbled, pushing the plate of sandwiches out of sight. 'I wasn't expecting you.'

'So it appears. Don't you ever have any clients to see?'

'We've already had two new ones this morning,' she informed him acidly.

'Business must be booming!' He looked round disparagingly. 'Does this place bring in enough to give both you and Miss Whitney a decent salary?'

'I've already explained that I don't work here on a permanent basis,' Natalie replied. 'I'm helping Maggie out while she's in hospital.' She hesitated. 'I'm on holiday from school.'

Sherry gold eyes appraised her. 'Don't tell me you're a teacher?'

'I wasn't going to tell you anything,' she said haughtily.

'What exactly do you teach?' he persisted.

'I'm a nursery school teacher.'

His mouth thinned. 'You don't look the type.'

'What type do I look?'

The glint in his eyes made her regret her question, and she spoke again quickly. 'Don't bother telling me, Mr Denton. I'm not interested in your opinion.'

'But you're interested in what I intend doing about this place, aren't you?' he said dryly. 'For someone who wants a favour from me, you're not very placatory.'

'Do you want me to beg?' she asked in a frigid voice. 'Or should I kneel in front of you? To be honest, Mr Denton, if it will help Maggie, I'm willing to do both.'

'Neither will be necessary,' he said in a clipped tone.

Without waiting to be asked, he sat down and crossed one long leg over the other. His shoes were highly polished and there was a glimpse of a black sock beneath the dark trousers. Despite it being a warm summer day, he had made no concession to the season but wore a crisp white shirt with a dark suit and tie. All he needed, she thought irritably, was a bowler hat and a tightly rolled umbrella. It would go well with his tight little character.

'I've decided to put you to the test,' he said without preamble. 'If you come out of it well, I'll overlook what happened to my sister.'

Natalie stared at him and waited for him to explain his use of the word 'test'. Surprisingly, he did not meet her eyes but fidgeted with the chair arm.

'It might be possible for this Agency to help *me*,' he said abruptly.

Natalie tried to hide her astonishment. To think a man like Miles Denton should require a marriage bureau! Still, it was not so surprising: he was probably an impossible man to love.

'We'll do our best to help you, Mr Denton,' she said sweetly. 'If you could tell me the age and type you're interested in meeting....'

For an instant he looked at her in blank astonishment, then he gave an irritable shake of his head.

'I don't require a wife, Miss Baker, but a husband for someone else. If I——'

'Your sister?'

'Don't you ever let anyone finish what they're going to say without interrupting them?' he asked forcefully.

Natalie had the grace to blush. 'I'm like that with the children,' she admitted. 'Some of them are a bit slow in telling me what they want, so....'

'I'm not a child, nor am I a bit slow,' he rejoined. 'And I would thank you to let me think and speak for myself.'

Resisting the urge to slap his thin, aristocratic-looking face, Natalie motioned him to continue.

'I wish to find a suitable masculine diversion for a young woman named Gayle Hunter,' he continued, and looked at Natalie as if he expected her to produce a suitable specimen immediately.

'I think you've come to the wrong place, Mr Denton. We're not an escort agency. We aim to find suitable *partners* for our clients, not diversions.'

'All the better if you found Gayle a husband,' he said instantly. 'But failing that, if you could at least divert her it would be of inestimable help to me. You've already met her,' he added laconically. 'She's the girl who arrived as you were leaving my house yesterday.'

Natalie hid her surprise. 'The baby-voiced blonde who got out of the taxi?'

He looked disconcerted by the description, and then nodded. 'That's the one.'

'I thought she was your girl-friend.'

'Unfortunately, so does she.'

This time Natalie's surprise showed on her face.

'I suppose I'd better begin at the beginning,' he sighed. 'Miss Hunter's mother and my own have been friends since they were schoolgirls, and from the time Gayle was born they've nourished the hope that we would grow up and marry each other. Unfortunately, it's an idea which has found great favour with Gayle.'

'But not with you?'

'Obviously not.'

'Then why not tell her?'

'I've tried to do so, but I can't seem to make her believe me.'

For a brief second Natalie thought he was joking, but the look on his face told her he was serious.

'Maybe you haven't been convincing enough,' she ventured. 'Perhaps you really love her.'

'I don't want to get married,' he replied. 'But I can't get her to believe me. She thinks herself in love with me.'

'How unfortunate for her!'

His mouth tightened. 'I don't expect you to understand, Miss Baker, though it might help if you were to try. After all, the continuation of your Agency depends on it.'

Seeing irritation on his face, Natalie folded her hands primly in her lap and looked at him with an air of sweet innocence.

'Please go on, Mr Denton.'

'I suppose you find this pretty amusing,' he said savagely, 'but I can assure you it's no joke to me. I'm contented with my present mode of life and have no wish to change its uncomplicated pattern for one of domesticity—no matter how blissful.'

'Perhaps you should be more blunt with Miss Hunter.'

'If I were any blunter it could well end her mother's friendship with my own, and that's something I'm loath to do. I've toyed with the idea of going out with other women, but in my profession that's impossible.'

'Why? You aren't a monk.'

His eyes narrowed into gold slits.

'You obviously don't realise the long hours I work. It leaves me little time for socialising, and even less inclination.'

'Are you a successful surgeon?' Natalie asked, and saw him give her an affronted look.

'Extremely.'

'Then if you're at the top, surely you can find a little more time for socialising?'

'Not quite the top, Miss Baker. In fact that's one reason why I'm reluctant to quarrel with Gayle.'

He paused and pulled at his ear lobe. It was an unexpectedly boyish gesture and Natalie felt her attitude towards him soften.

'Much as I want to get Gayle out of my life,' he continued, 'it would be most embarrassing for me to have an outright row with her.'

'Because of your mothers.' Natalie reminded him that he had already told her the story.

'And also because of Gayle's father,' he said stiffly. 'I'm being considered for the position of Senior Consultant at my hospital, and the man stepping down from the post—and who can recommend me for it—is Sir Elton Hunter.'

Natalie's sympathy vanished. This last statement made sense of what, until now, she had found incomprehensible. She had never believed Miles Denton to be incapable of making his opinions known. In that respect he was as concise as the Oxford Dictionary. No, he wanted to be rid of Gayle Hunter without doing any harm to his career.

'I still don't see how this agency can help you,' she said.

'I've just told you I want Gayle to meet other men —ones who like the same sort of things she does—dancing, tennis, skiing. She might then realise I'm not the only fish in the sea.'

'Why don't you simply make yourself unavailable?' Natalie asked.

'I thought I'd made it clear why I don't want to quarrel with her.'

'Because of Sir Elton,' Natalie said waspishly.

'Because of her mother's friendship with my own,' he corrected.

Natalie stared at him and he looked back at her as though defying her to argue with him. She wondered if he believed what he was saying, or whether he could not bring himself to admit that it was his unwillingness to annoy Sir Elton that was making him act so out of character towards a girl who, as far as she could tell, was a designing young woman.

She wished now that she had paid greater attention to the girl, but could remember nothing apart from a baby voice and long-legged grace.

'I'm afraid we can't put Miss Hunter on our books. She must come here herself and enrol,' she said.

'I'm glad to find you are so scrupulous,' Miles Denton said unpleasantly. 'But please remember that your licence will be revoked if you don't help me.'

Natalie leaned back in her chair and looked at him.

'You're very *un*scrupulous, Mr Denton.'

'I'm a determined man, Miss Baker.'

Determined to rid himself of a threat to his bachelor status without causing a threat to his career! Natalie thought of him in the operating theatre and found it easy to envisage him wielding a knife.

'What are you thinking?' he asked abruptly.

'How well you would wield a scalpel,' she said without evasion.

The expulsion of his breath was audible and his eyes blazed with anger, reminding her of the man who had come into her office yesterday.

'The choice is yours, Miss Baker,' he said. 'The Agency helps—or the Agency closes. I will expect you at Harley Street at six o'clock this evening with a list of men whom you consider suitable.'

Natalie swallowed her own anger. 'How will Miss Hunter meet them? I've already told you she has to enrol here personally.'

'Find me a few suitable men for her, and I'll figure something out.'

'I don't even know the sort of men she likes,' Natalie went on desperately.

'Men like me.'

'We don't have such paragons on our books!'

Miles Denton scowled but ignored the comment. 'Gayle's twenty-two. She went to boarding school in Switzerland; she's an excellent athlete and loves dancing, travelling and meeting people.' He paused. 'Is there anything else you need to know?'

'What size shoes does she wear?'

Finely arched eyebrows met above Miles Denton's long, straight nose. 'I'll see you at my rooms at six,' he said, and without waiting for her reply, walked out.

CHAPTER FOUR

NATALIE knew she had no option but to do as Miles Denton had asked. He was the piper who called the tune and she was forced to dance to it.

Diligently she searched through the list of men who might be eligible to introduce to Gayle Hunter, but they were dismally few. Young men who would appeal to such a lovely-looking creature were not likely to be found on the books of a marriage bureau, any more than one would find such a girl enrolling. This made her wonder again what had brought the surgeon's sister on to their books. From all accounts, Gillian Denton was equally eyecatching. It was a pity she had not asked Roland; he was bound to know. Still, the less she spoke to him about Gillian the better.

Armed at last with the necessary list—a sparse one but all she could muster—Natalie stood on the steps of the house in Harley Street and pressed the bell marked *Visitors*. It was exactly six o'clock and she hoped Mr Denton would appreciate her punctuality. There was no answer and, after a moment, she pressed the bell again, wondering hopefully whether the man had had second thoughts about his request. But if he had, surely he would not let her call here on a false errand?

She was debating whether to ring for the third time when the door was flung back and she found herself looking at a girl a few years her junior.

Natalie's first thought was that Miles Denton seemed

to be surrounded by beautiful young women, for this one, though different in type from Gayle Hunter, was equally pretty. She had light brown hair and tawny eyes with incredibly long lashes. It was obvious from the open bar of chocolate she held in her hand that she was quite at home here.

'Mr Denton is expecting me,' Natalie said.

'Are you Miss Baker?'

'Yes.'

The girl opened the door wider. 'Mrs Evans told me you were expected and I promised to show you upstairs. She's generally here until six o'clock, but she wasn't feeling well, so I sent her off early.'

Still speaking, the girl led the way to a small lift.

'Are you a friend of Miles? I haven't seen you around before. But then I'm not here as often as I used to be. I once had my own key and could get in when I liked, but then Miles went and changed all the locks.'

'Should you be telling me this?' Natalie asked, faintly discomfited.

For an instant the girl looked surprised, then she flung back her head and laughed. 'Good lord, I'm not his girl-friend, I'm his sister!'

Natalie couldn't help smiling. So this was Gillian Denton. She could suddenly see the likeness, and found it incredible that the girl should have come to the Whitney Marriage Bureau.

'How long have you known Miles?' Gillian Denton asked, opening the door of the lift and following Natalie in.

'I'm not a friend of his. I'm—I'm a business acquaintance.'

Gillian's sherry gold eyes appraised her. They were remarkably like her brother's, Natalie thought.

'How intriguing,' the girl asked. 'Are you a nurse or a doctor?'

'I'm a nursery school teacher.'

'You don't look it,' Gillian replied. 'I wouldn't have patience with children. Miles says I don't have patience for anything, but then he's rather hard on me.'

The lift stopped at the third floor and they got out. They made their way along a thickly carpeted corridor and Gillian opened the door of a large sitting-room. Deep-piled white carpet lay wall to wall, and upon it stood several armchairs and a low chesterfield, covered in deep blue velvet. Silk-draped walls were smothered with an abundance of highly coloured modern paintings, all abstract, and the tall windows were softened by drapes whose material picked out the more dominant colours of the large Mark Rothko above the matelshelf.

'How different from the waiting room downstairs!' Natalie exclaimed.

'Gayle did the decor for this one,' Gillian explained, and then looked embarrassed. 'Do you—er—know her?'

'I know of her.'

'Thank goodness for that! Miles is always telling me off for being indiscreet.'

Natalie hid a smile, knowing that Gillian still assumed her to be her brother's girl-friend.

'Gayle wants to have a go at the waiting room next,' the girl went on, 'but Miles has managed to put her off.'

'Why?'

'Because he absolutely loathes the way she did *this* room, and he's too polite to say so.'

It was impossible for Natalie to imagine the surgeon being polite to anyone, until she remembered he would not wish to be rude to the daughter of the man who could chop off the next step of the ladder he wished to climb.

She sat down on one of the easy chairs and looked at her watch.

'Will your brother be long?'

'Depends on the patient. I know it's his last one.' Gillian Denton perched on the arm of a chair and idly swung a shapely leg. 'Are you sure you aren't a personal friend of Miles?' she questioned. 'It would be one in the eye for Gayle if you were.'

'I can assure you I'm not,' Natalie smiled. 'Though I must admit I know what you mean.'

'Good. Much as I could sometimes kill my brother, I would hate to see him married to that pseud. Once he put the ring on her finger she'd take it off and try to put it through his nose!'

'Really?' Natalie questioned, hoping to hear more.

Gillian leaned forward. 'In my opinion she's nowhere as dumb as she makes out.'

'A lot of girls put on that sort of act.'

'Try telling it to Miles and he'll bite your head off. He may be a brilliant surgeon—he *is* brilliant, in fact —but he's a dimwit where women are concerned. The only time he understands a woman is when she's unconscious on the operating table in front of him!'

Natalie burst out laughing and after a second the other girl joined in. But the laughter stopped abruptly as the door opened and the object of their mirth faced them.

'Goodbye, Gilly,' he said abruptly.

'Do you want me to go?' his sister asked artlessly, and getting to her feet, flung Natalie a look of amusement before bouncing out of the room.

'I take it my sister doesn't know why you are here or who you are?' he said in a voice devoid of expression, yet managing to convey disapproval.

'No, she doesn't,' Natalie said abruptly.

'Good. She's as discreet as a Sunday tabloid.'

'But far more innocent,' Natalie flashed, and for the first time saw a genuine smile cross his face.

It made a remarkable difference to him, and she realised that he was not only young but also very good-looking.

'Would you like a drink?' he asked.

'No, thank you.' She was sorry the moment she had answered, for his face took on its sharp look again as he sat down on the settee.

'May I change my mind,' she murmured, 'and have a gin and tonic?'

Immediately he rose and crossed to the sideboard in the far corner. She watched his hands moving deftly as he poured the drinks. They were long, beautifully shaped hands that suddenly made her see him as a man who saved lives. She remembered the sarcasm that had waged between them and felt cheapened by it. If only she could have met him in more normal circumstances!

'Miss Baker?'

With a start she saw he was standing in front of her, proffering a glass. She took it.

'I assume you've been able to do as I asked?' he said questioningly.

She nodded, and wished fleetingly that he had not made it so obvious that he wanted her to say what she had to say and be gone.

'I hope I can help you,' she murmured. 'As I said earlier, we don't have many young men on our books, but I've brought you a list of those that are available.'

She opened her bag and took out a typewritten list. Miles Denton had resumed his seat beside her and was nursing a whisky tumbler between his long flexible fingers.

'Go on,' he said quietly. 'Give me a run-down of them.'

She began to do so, and it was some fifteen minutes before she stopped and looked at him. He was resting his head against the settee and a soft lock of hair had fallen across his forehead. He was more relaxed than she had ever seen him and his normally pale skin was whisky-warm. Again she wished they had met in different circumstances, and was dismayed that she should be thinking like this. Determinedly she pushed the thought away and spoke.

'Which of the men do you like, Mr Denton?'

'None.'

'Surely the architect——'

'He's far too old for Gayle. Anyway, he's been divorced, and her parents would never approve.'

'What about Steve Loring, the engineer?'

'Gayle doesn't like men who wear glasses.' He jumped up. 'They're all hopeless. You must do better than that.'

'I've already combed the books,' she stated.

'Then comb them again. I thought I made it quite clear the sort of man I wanted.'

'Oh, you did,' she scoffed. 'A facsimile of yourself. But that's quite impossible, Mr Denton. They don't make many men like you.'

'Spare me your sarcasm, Miss Baker.'

The unusual edginess which Natalie had been experiencing for the last half hour suddenly erupted into a blaze of temper she was totally unable to control.

'I wasn't being sarcastic, Mr Denton. They *don't* make many men like you—and thank goodness for that! If you want to find Miss Hunter a replacement for yourself, then you'd better go to Madame Tussauds and ask them to make an effigy of you—because I don't think there's a marriage bureau in the world that will have anyone as wonderful as you on their books!'

There was a lengthy silence, during which Miles Denton set down his glass and folded his arms across his chest.

'I'm glad you appreciate my worth, Miss Baker. You're a woman of perception.'

Natalie refused to rise to the bait. 'I've given you a complete list of everyone that's anywhere near suitable,' she said coldly, 'and you've turned them all down. We're not a big bureau, Mr Denton, and I can't find clients out of thin air.'

'What about your own boy-friends?'

Incredulously she stared at him.

'My own boy-friends?'

'You do have some, I assume.' His eyes moved over her, from the top of her russet brown hair, past the full curve of her breasts and small waist, to the shapely hips that lengthened into slender legs. 'You do have boy-friends?' he repeated.

Indignantly she glared at him. 'You're not suggesting I introduce them to Miss Hunter, are you?'

'Why not? I wouldn't expect you to introduce her to anyone of whom you're particularly fond.'

'Thanks,' she said dryly, and noticed a glint in the back of his eyes that made her wonder how serious his suggestion had been.

'Do you really mean it, Mr Denton? About my producing my own boy-friends?'

He shrugged. 'If you know of anyone suitable, what would be the harm in getting them together? We could always go out in a foursome one evening.'

'It's quite out of the question!' Natalie's cheeks burned, and as she tried to regain her composure, the suggestion he had made fired another one in her own mind. 'Since I can't find anyone for Miss Hunter, why don't we try to find someone for *you*? I know you don't want to get involved with another woman, but you could perhaps pretend long enough for Miss Hunter to get the message.'

'And how do you suggest I get rid of this female when I no longer want to pretend?'

'I'm sure you wouldn't find it difficult, Mr Denton. Your hands are only tied with Miss Hunter because of her father.'

In the silence that met her remark, she heard the whine of the lift, followed by the clanging of a door and light footsteps coming along the corridor.

'Miles!' a soft voice called. 'Miles darling, I'm here!'

With a swift glance at the surgeon, Natalie braced herself for the look of surprise which she knew she would see on Gayle Hunter's face as she stepped into the sitting-room and saw 'Miles darling' with the same redhead she had seen yesterday.

It all happened so exactly as Natalie envisaged that she was hard put to it not to laugh.

'I didn't know you were still busy, darling,' Gayle said reproachfully, then looked directly at Natalie. 'We've met before, I think.'

Natalie nodded but did not vouchsafe any information. Let Miles Denton get out of this predicament as best he could!

'Miss Baker is a friend of mine,' he said, crossing to the sideboard. 'Your usual, Gayle?'

'Thank you, darling.' She glided over to him as he took half a bottle of champagne from an ice bucket, and deftly opened it. He glanced round at Natalie.

'Would you care for a glass?' he asked.

'No, thanks, I must be going.'

'Don't mind me,' said Gayle. 'If you two have any business to talk over I'll just sit quietly and relax.'

'Our business is finished,' said Natalie, rising to leave. 'Don't bother seeing me down,' she said quickly as Miles Denton followed her to the door. 'I can find my own way out.'

Not giving him a chance to reply, she hurried to the lift. Behind her she heard Gayle's voice, high and amused as she spoke, uncaring whether or not Natalie would hear her.

'I thought you didn't like big girls, darling. Though I'll admit she's very colourful. What bright hair!'

Carefully Natalie closed the door of the lift, but gave the bell a savage press, and was still seething with temper as she stepped out on to the ground floor. She was at the front door when she heard swift steps pounding down the stairs, and turning her head, she saw Miles Denton striding towards her.

'I'm glad I caught you,' he said breathlessly, and paused to draw air into his lungs. 'I really must take more exercise. I'm always telling my patients to do so, but I never follow my own instructions.'

'Doctors generally don't.'

He gave a half smile and then became serious. 'I

think you came up with an excellent idea a moment ago, Miss Baker.'

She was at a loss. 'What idea?'

'That you should find someone for *me* instead of for Gayle. I do see it would be difficult for you to introduce her to anyone who would compare favourably with myself.'

Natalie stared at him, and his expression told her he was mocking her.

'Go on,' she said darkly. 'What devious plot are you hatching now?'

'Something I should have hatched yesterday, if I'd had any sense. I want Gayle to believe I've fallen madly in love with another woman.'

'When I suggested it, you said——'

'I know what I said,' he interrupted. 'But I didn't want to get involved with another woman in case I jumped out of the frying pan into the fire. But with *you*, there wouldn't be any fire.'

'What have I got to do with it?' she asked, knowing instantly what he meant, but refusing to admit it.

'I'm going to pretend I'm in love with *you*,' he said with satisfaction. 'You saw the way Gayle reacted when she found you upstairs. It's the ideal solution.'

'On the contrary, it's absolutely ridiculous!'

'Why? What harm will it do to pretend for a few weeks?'

'You won't fool her,' she assured him.

'I've already fooled her. She's absolutely furious because I raced down after you. It will be the easiest thing in the world to make her believe I've fallen for you.' Miles Denton looked very pleased with himself. 'I'm sure I'll be able to put on a convincing act.'

'Unfortunately I won't,' Natalie said tartly.

'You'll have to try, Miss Baker. My mind's made up. After all, you yourself suggested this solution.'

'When I said you should find another girl-friend, I didn't mean me.'

'What's wrong with you? It would be extremely unfair to introduce me to a bona fide client, bearing in mind that I've no intention of getting married. You're the ideal stand-in, Miss Baker.'

'And what will happen when our pretended love affair ends and Miss Hunter walks back into your life?'

'I'm hoping her pride won't let her.'

'If she loves you, she won't let pride stand in her way. It wouldn't stop *me*.'

'You're a different type from Gayle.'

'Luckily for you,' she said, and pulling open the door, hurried out into the street.

Effortlessly the man kept pace with her.

'I'll see you tomorrow,' he said. 'Be here at the same time.'

'What for?'

'So we can begin our love affair.'

'Never!'

'It's only pretence,' he assured her. 'Either you do as I ask or——'.

'I don't want to hear,' she said furiously. 'If it weren't for Maggie....'

A vacant taxi cruised by and she signalled it to stop. Miles Denton opened the door for her and she climbed in, then looked at him through the open window.

'I live at 18 Kidderminster Terrace,' she said softly. 'It's the top floor flat. I'll expect you at eight.'

'But——'

'It's usual for the gentleman to call for the lady,' she said sweetly, 'so don't be late—Miles darling!'

CHAPTER FIVE

THE taxi took Natalie straight from Harley Street to the hospital, where Maggie was looking distinctly peaky after her operation.

'I'm afraid I won't be out of here as quickly as I'd hoped,' she confessed. 'Angus says there were a few complications and I'll need some extra treatment.'

'It's not the end of the world,' Natalie said in a rallying tone. 'I'm coping beautifully at the office. We've even had some new clients today.'

'Honestly?'

'Honestly. I took down all the particulars, and one of the clients—a divorced man of fifty—says he knows lots of other men who'd be happy to come to us, once we'd got *him* settled.'

Maggie brightened. 'There's no shortage of women on our books. If you need me to advise you, bring some of the cards in with you tomorrow.'

'Not on your life,' Natalie said firmly. '*I'm* running the business for the moment, and I can manage without your advice.'

Maggie leaned back against the pillows. 'I don't know what I'd have done without you. You're an angel, Natalie.'

'And you'd have become one if you hadn't been taken to hospital. You're a clot, Maggie. Don't you know that being well is more important than anything else?'

'I do now,' Maggie admitted, and looked paler than

ever. 'Roland hasn't been to see me today.'

'Nor me,' said Natalie, and then decided to be blunt. 'I told him not to come in to the office. We rub each other the wrong way.'

'Do you know what he's doing?' Maggie looked worried.

'No. But he said he had one or two things in the offing and I gave him some money—fifty pounds.'

Maggie frowned. 'I didn't leave you any signed cheques.'

'So what? I can always lay out my own money and you can pay me back afterwards.'

'They must be paying teachers more than I realised,' Maggie smiled. 'You really should start your own nursery school.'

'At the moment I'm more concerned with your marriage bureau. I find the work fascinating.'

For the remainder of the visiting time Natalie regaled her friend with gossip and was relieved to see Maggie lose some of her listlessness. Natalie was the last visitor to leave the ward, and only as she reached the corridor did she realise how hungry she was. She quickened her pace and rounded a corner so abruptly that she ran full tilt into a muscular body that, disengaging itself from her, turned out to be Maggie's friend Angus.

He frowned down at her, then suddenly smiled. 'You're Natalie, aren't you?'

'That's right. And you're just the man I wanted to see. I'd like to know how Maggie is.'

'Haven't you seen her?'

'Of course. But I want a professional opinion.'

'She's as well as can be expected.' He saw Natalie's expression and grinned. 'When I was a student I vowed I would never give stock answers like that, and here I am doing it!' He moved closer to the wall in order not to be in the way of oncoming people, and Natalie followed him.

'Actually, Maggie's had a pretty rough time,' he continued. 'She'll be here another two weeks at least, and after that she'll need to convalesce for a month.'

'As long as that?'

'If possible. Will you be able to help her out for that length of time?'

'Just about. I start school again in five weeks. I don't know what Maggie will do if you won't let her begin work by then.'

'She'll have to close the business until she's better.'

'That may not be so easy to do,' Natalie warned. 'The office is small, but the rent isn't.'

A frown marked Angus's face and he looked like a worried bulldog.

'We'll have to try and think of something,' he muttered. 'But meanwhile I don't want Maggie worried.'

'Nor do I,' Natalie assured him, 'so I'm keeping the problems to myself.'

'Are there many?' he asked.

Natalie hesitated before replying.

'Do you know Maggie's brother Roland?'

'We were at school together. That's how I first met Maggie. I never liked him very much.'

'Then you'd like him even less now.'

'Is he still looking for the easy buck?'

'And the easy doe,' Natalie said dryly, and briefly told Angus what had happened with Gillian Denton.

During the recital Angus steered her into the cafeteria, where he plied her with coffee and sticky buns and listened attentively to the whole story.

'I never realised Mr Denton was such an oddball,' he said as she finished.

Only then did Natalie realise how indiscreet she had been. Miles Denton was, after all, in the same profession as Angus.

'He isn't odd at all,' she amended hastily. 'He just finds it difficult to cope with designing women—one in particular, anyway.'

'I've seen Gayle Hunter around,' Angus said. 'She's a dish, though evidently not to Denton's taste.'

'I don't think he wants to get married to anyone.'

'Awkward for him. Old Hunter's retiring soon and rumour has it that Denton will be taking his place. I can see why he doesn't want to offend the old boy by turning down his daughter.'

Natalie nodded, and again wished she had not blabbered to the extent she had done. But it was too late to retract anything.

'Using me as a red herring was just an idea of his,' she explained.

'Some herring!' Angus grinned. 'But it won't work. I'm not much of a psychologist, but even I know that the worst thing possible to do with a girl like Gayle is to bring another woman on the scene. Far from leaving him, she'll be more determined than ever to hook him.'

Natalie was annoyed she had not thought of this herself, particularly as she was a woman who should have known how somebody like Gayle would react. But she had been so disturbed by Miles Denton's threats that she had been unable to think clearly; and now, of course, it was too late to tell him, for she had already committed herself to do as he wanted.

'You won't tell Maggie what's going on, will you?' she implored.

'Not a word. And if Roland comes in, I'll make sure he doesn't say anything either.'

'Roland doesn't know that I've agreed to help Mr Denton,' Natalie said hastily. 'I told him not to hang around the office and I haven't seen him since. For God's sake don't mention any of this to him.'

Promising to be the soul of discretion, Angus parted from Natalie at the hospital door, and she returned to her flat wondering if a romance could be blossoming between Angus and Maggie. How wonderful if Maggie lost a gall bladder and found a husband! It seemed an excellent exchange and one she would not mind for herself. But not with Angus, of course. She thought of the raw-boned Scot and found the image superseded by a tall, austere figure with wide shoulders. It was such a startling thought that she hurriedly went into her little kitchen to make herself some supper. She had not eaten since lunch and was obviously becoming lightheaded.

But even when sustained by wholemeal bread and two boiled eggs, she still could not get Miles Denton out of her mind. Being angry with a man made one think of him far too much, she decided, and she wished wholeheartedly that she had never set eyes on him.

In the morning she awoke with a vague feeling of irritability. It accompanied her to the office and made her deal almost sharply with the telephone calls that came in.

'I don't know why you should be so annoyed with me because I don't like Mr Rogers,' came a plaintive comment from one client.

Conceding that the woman was right, Natalie forced herself into a calmer frame of mind. She was here to help Maggie keep the agency going; not to let her own irritation with Miles Denton bring about its demise.

'I'm terribly sorry, Miss Peebles,' she placated. 'It's just that we thought Mr Rogers was so suitable for you. But if you don't like him, we'll introduce you to someone else.'

By lunchtime Natalie's equilibrium was totally restored. She had enrolled two further new clients and felt affluent enough to ring down to the café and ask them to send her up a pot of coffee and a salad.

As she began eating, the telephone rang again, and she swallowed a mouthful of salami and said hello.

'Miles Denton here.'

It was the first time Natalie had heard him speak without seeing him, and it made her more conscious of the deepness of his voice. She could imagine how reassuring it would be to hear when one was waking up from an anaesthetic. She shook her head, as if to clear it of such a stupid thought, and said sweetly:

'Have you rung up to tell me you've changed your mind, Mr Denton?'

'I'm ringing to say I'd like to call for you at seven. I've managed to get tickets for the new musical at the Regency Theatre.'

Natalie was surprised by his choice. Though the reviews for the show had been good, she would have assumed him to have preferred something more cerebral.

'I found out this morning that Sir Elton is taking his family to see the show tonight,' Miles Denton went on, making it clear why he had got the tickets. 'I thought it would be an excellent opportunity to parade our association.'

She grinned at the receiver. He made the word 'association' sound so lurid.

'Do you want me to wear a scarlet dress?' she asked guilelessly.

There was a short silence.

'It would clash with your hair.'

'What about green?' she suggested. 'That might echo the colour of Miss Hunter's face when she sees me with you.'

There was another silence, broken this time by his giving an unmistakable chuckle.

'Wear anything you like, Miss Baker. You're naturally voluptuous and will look it, even in a potato sack.'

Natalie remembered this comment as she searched through her wardrobe that evening. Despite his determination to remain unmarried, Mr Denton had a subtle way of paying a compliment. But then why should that be surprising? Because a man wished to remain free, it did not mean he also wanted to live the life of a celibate.

She was still pondering on this, as well as on what to wear, when the doorbell rang. With her heart beating at an unaccountable pace, she slipped into a housecoat and hurried to open the door.

Miles Denton stepped into the small hallway. The darkness of his dinner jacket made him look even more austere than usual, and she could imagine him putting the fear of death into some nervous young student nurse. Then he smiled at her, and Natalie immediately revised her opinion and wondered how she could have forgotten the heart-stopping colour of sherry gold eyes.

Quickly stepping back, she led him into the sitting-room.

'Help yourself to a drink, Mr Denton. I won't be long.'

'I don't want a drink, thanks.'

He went to stand by the mantelshelf. The mirror behind him reflected the back of his head and she noticed he wore his hair longer than she had thought. It was thick hair, and a warmer shade of brown than she had remembered.

'Will you be ready soon?' he asked.

'I only have to put on my dress.'

'What's wrong with the one you're wearing?'

She looked down at her long blue housecoat and then up at him, not sure if he was joking. But his expression told her he was serious, and she could not help laughing.

'As an evening dress, this is very Orphan Annie! Wait till you see me in the real thing. It's guaranteed to make Miss Hunter give up the fight!'

'Excellent.'

His tone was dry, but there was a glint in his eyes that made Natalie decide he had a sense of humour. A deeply buried one, it seemed, but there, nonetheless.

'You'd better hurry,' he said quietly. 'I don't want us to be late.'

She went swiftly into her bedroom and put on a mint green dress. It was one of her nicest and she had not intended to wear it. But something had made her change her mind, though what that something was she refused to analyse.

But the reason confronted her when she returned to the other room, though to her chagrin Miles Denton made no comment on her appearance. But his cool appraisal of her awakened her to the transparency of the silk chiffon that covered her shoulders and arms, placing a film of hazy green over the peachy glow of her skin. Although not low-cut, the delicate ruffle of material that lay across her breasts moved tantalisingly as she breathed, drawing attention to the full curves they hid.

She was gripped by nervousness—as she always seemed to be when she was with him—and told herself it had nothing to do with the man as such, but with what he represented: a threat to Maggie's livelihood.

Determinedly she gazed at him, willing herself to be calm. He was still viewing her with detachment, and she decided he was so used to seeing women in varying states of undress that one more made no difference to him, especially one whom he was taking out merely as a means to an end. But not the end that a young, virile male usually had in mind, she thought, humour getting the better of her, but as an end to Gayle Hunter.

'Ready?' he enquired and, at her nod, led her down to his car.

It was not the sedate saloon she had expected, but was low-slung and rakish. In the closeness of its interior she was even more aware of him as a man than an aloof surgeon. He drove surprisingly fast but competently, and knowing he was giving all his attention to the road, she was able to study him at length. In profile his features appeared highly chiselled, which lent an austerity to his expression. There might well be a man of deep feeling beneath the façade, but one would have to dig a long way in order to find it.

'How long have you been a surgeon?' she asked.

'I beg your pardon?'

She hid a smile at his startled tone. 'It's not that I'm greatly interested in you, Mr Denton,' she lied with candour, 'but if I'm supposed to be your girlfriend, I should know a little bit about you, don't you think?'

'Of course.' He spoke fast. 'I don't take sugar in coffee, nor do I like it with milk. I rarely drink tea. I have a fondness for wine—red in preference to white—and I always have two whiskies when I come home in the evening. Is that the sort of thing a girl-friend should know?'

'Do you wear pyjamas in bed?'

The car jerked slightly.

'Yes,' he said. 'But only the jacket. What about you?'

Colour came and went in her cheeks, but she knew she deserved the question.

'I don't wear pyjamas, and my nightdresses are more utilitarian than glamorous.'

'You have a natural glamour, Miss Baker,' he said prosaically. 'You have a beautiful face and an excellent figure.'

'I have all my own teeth too,' she said brightly.

'Perhaps I'll be able to ascertain that for myself at a more auspicious time.'

His answer was pat and this time the colour came into her cheeks and stayed there.

'By the way,' he said abruptly, 'I don't know your first name.'

'Natalie.'

He nodded, then slowed the car and stopped. Looking through the window, she was surprised to see they were outside his house in Harley Street.

'I thought we were going to the theatre?' she exclaimed.

'It's impossibly difficult to park in the West End,' he replied, helping her out and locking the doors with amazing speed. 'This way it's far less bother,' he added, flagging down a cruising taxi and ushering her in. 'We'll come back here afterwards and I can drive you home.'

'Thank you.'

'Don't mention it,' he said politely. 'You're doing me a great favour.'

'Am I?' She looked at him steadily. 'I had the impression I was being ordered to obey you under duress.'

He did not answer, but something prevented her from letting the subject drop.

'What made your sister come to the Whitney Bureau, Mr Denton? I can't imagine her having any difficulty in finding boy-friends.'

He was silent for so long that she was sure he was not going to answer, but eventually he did.

'It was my fault that she went. Since she was seventeen she's been falling in and out of love with the most impossible young men. The last time she created a bit more havoc than I could tolerate, and I warned her that if she didn't behave herself I would cut her allowance.'

'Doesn't she work?'

'Fitfully. She has an income from a trust fund which I manage for her, and it's far more than she needs. I'm her guardian until she's twenty-five, which is another reason why she likes to provoke me.'

'You still haven't said why she went to a marriage bureau.'

'It was because I suggested she stop wasting her time with hippies and Maoists. In a temper she went to see your friend and, as far as I can gather, gave her a description of a man whom she thought would meet with my approval. The next thing that happened was that she received a call from Roland Whitney. The rest you know.'

'Not quite. Only that your sister bought him some cufflinks and that you found out when he went to sell them.'

'The cufflinks were the last in a long line of presents,' he said tonelessly. 'He took money from her too. Apparently he spun her a yarn about being short of cash.'

'How did you find out about the links?' Natalie asked curiously.

'My sister bought them at the family jewellers and pretended she was buying them for me. When Whitney took them back to sell them, they assumed he had stolen them—which in a way he had—and they kept him there while they contacted me.'

'What did you do?'

The beautifully tailored jacket moved as the man's shoulders lifted in a shrug of helplessness. 'I told them they weren't mine and that they must do as they pleased. A scandal was the last thing I wanted. However, I tackled Gillian and got the whole story from her. That's when I decided to come and see you.'

'To see the Whitney Marriage Bureau,' Natalie corrected. 'I'm only helping Maggie on a temporary basis.'

'But you take her wellbeing very much to heart, don't you?' he said.

'She's as important to me as your good name is to you,' Natalie replied stolidly. 'Otherwise I wouldn't be here with you now.'

'I appreciate why you're doing it, Miss Baker, and I promise you that if you don't let me down, your friend will have nothing to worry about.'

'As long as you promise not to blame me if you don't fool Miss Hunter,' she said quickly.

His lids blinked rapidly. 'I don't follow you.'

'Miss Hunter may not be put off by your having another girl-friend. In fact, it could make her all the more keen.'

'Surely not?'

'Wouldn't it make you keener if someone you liked

went out with another man?'

'No,' he said incisively. 'If I were ever foolish enough to fall in love and the girl didn't have the good sense to——'

Natalie's giggle cut him short and he looked at her affrontedly. 'What's funny about that?'

'Everything. You're unbelievable, Mr Denton. If I thought you ever had a chance of marrying, I'd be sorry for your wife.'

'It's purely because I have more than a chance,' he said quietly, 'that you happen to be here tonight. And please don't call me Mr Denton in front of Sir Elton and his wife.'

'Don't worry, *darling*,' said Natalie, choking back another giggle, 'I'll coo at you like a dove.'

The taxi stopped and she saw they were at the theatre. Courteously he handed her out and escorted her into the foyer.

'Natalie,' he said in her ear, and she stopped so abruptly that she bumped into him.

'What is it?'

'Nothing. I was just rehearsing your name.' His eyes looked into hers and the wall lights around the foyer were reflected in them. 'Five years,' he said softly.

'Five years?' she repeated uncomprehendingly, not sure if he meant her mental age or whether he anticipated using her services for that length of time.

'Since I became a surgeon,' he explained.

'How old are you?'

'Thirty-five.'

'You look older.'

'Thanks!'

'That's because you behave so stuffily!'

His hand came out and caught her arm. She expected him to make some sharp comeback, but instead he relaxed his grip, though he still retained his hold on her. Through her fine folds of chiffon she felt the gentleness of his fingertips, their touch as light as a feather, yet strangely firm and reassuring.

'The last bell has gone,' he murmured. 'We must go in.'

They moved unhurriedly to their seats and settled down. Natalie let out a sigh. The play she was about to see promised to be far less exciting than the one in which she and Miles Denton were participating.

CHAPTER SIX

ALTHOUGH the musical was brash, it had catchy tunes and an earthy humour, and Natalie discovered that Miles Denton's laugh was completely uninhibited.

'This is a rare luxury for me,' he said, as the curtain came down on the first act. 'I rarely finish before seven-thirty in the evening.'

'I thought surgeons only operated in the morning.'

'In the afternoon I see patients,' he explained with a slight smile. 'I also have to go round the wards. Hospital work involves long hours.'

'But you enjoy it?'

'Oh yes. I could have more free time if I wished,' he admitted, 'but my work is also my pleasure. I do try to keep my weekends free, though. I often go and stay with my mother in the country. She lives near Aylesbury.'

Natalie's curiosity was aroused, but she did not want him to think she was interested in him and deliberately refrained from asking him any more. Although he was relaxed and chatting easily, she sensed his fatigue and noticed the fine lines at the corners of his eyes, and the more deeply etched ones at the sides of his mouth.

'What time did you start operating today?' she asked.

He looked taken aback at her question, but answered it. 'Eight o'clock. I expected to finish at noon, but I had an emergency that took three hours, so I didn't leave the theatre until half-past two.'

He would then have done his rounds of the wards

and no doubt a hundred and one other things, Natalie thought, knowing it would have done him far more good to have gone home, taken a bath and stepped right into bed. Yet if she said as much, how surprised he would be by her solicitude; almost as surprised as she was to experience it.

'We're being watched,' he murmured, and gave her a tender smile as if he were whispering sweet nothings into her ear.

'Where?' she whispered back.

'On your left, but for heaven's sake don't turn around.'

It was an effort not to do so, for she would have liked to have seen Gayle Hunter's face.

'I'm sure we'll be invited to have a drink with Sir Elton during the interval,' Miles said.

'Won't he be annoyed to see you here with me?' Natalie questioned.

'His attitude will depend on how charming you are to him.'

The answer was quick and cool, as if thought had already been given to it.

'If you can persuade Sir Elton of your beauty and intelligence, he might be more understanding of my fall from grace!'

'I won't need to convince him of my beauty,' Natalie said smoothly. 'He's a man and can see that for himself. But it might be difficult to convince him of my intelligence. Only a fool would go out with you!'

Tawny eyes glittered. 'You're never at a loss for a reply, are you, my *darling*?'

'Think how disappointed you would be if I were!'

They walked up the aisle towards the bar and Natalie was conscious of the many admiring glances they drew; male eyes drawn to her own sparkling beauty, and female ones intrigued by the aloof detachment of her highly personable escort. She wondered what it would feel like to be out with him because he wanted to be with her, and felt unexpectedly depressed to know this was not the case now.

'Here we go,' he whispered, and cupping her elbow with his hand he urged her towards the tall, grey-haired man standing beside a woman who was an older version of Gayle. Gayle herself looked exceptionally pretty. Her long blonde hair was pulled back from her face and she wore a Grecian style dress in white jersey silk which made her look much taller than she was.

'Natalie, I'd like you to meet Sir Elton and Lady Hunter. Gayle, of course, you already know.'

Natalie smiled at the older couple and more briefly at Gayle, who returned it with a look of smouldering dislike before speaking to Miles.

'You didn't tell me you were coming to the theatre tonight.' Her voice was quiet but penetrating.

'Natalie got the tickets at the last moment,' Miles said, lying with an ease that Natalie found astonishing.

'Your taste is different from Gayle's, then,' Sir Elton said to her. 'She only came with us tonight because it's our twenty-third wedding anniversary.'

'I'm not really keen on this type of show,' Natalie admitted, 'but I think it's a good way of helping Miles to relax. Much more so than if he'd concentrated on some deep play with a message.'

'I think one can relax even if one concentrates,' said Lady Hunter. 'Bridge is a prime example.'

'I'm afraid I don't play bridge,' Natalie smiled.

'You'd better learn if you want to see much of Miles,' Gayle said waspishly. 'You haven't forgotten you're making a foursome with us tomorrow night, have you?'

'Of course not,' Miles replied, and then looked directly at Natalie. 'I did tell you I was playing bridge tomorrow, didn't I, sweetie?'

'Why, yes,' she replied, only just managing to hide her astonishment at his casual tone.

A waiter approached with a tray of drinks, and Natalie accepted a glass of champagne and waited while Miles toasted the anniversary couple.

'It's time you thought of marriage too, Miles,' said Lady Hunter. 'And Gayle as well,' she added. 'Your mother and I were talking about the two of you only yesterday.'

'And the day before that too, I'll be bound,' said her husband. 'That's all you and Ailsa talk about. These things can't be rushed. The children will get married in their own time.'

Natalie sipped her champagne and kept firmly out of the conversation, silently applauding Miles for maintaining an innocent expression and the way in which he then managed to change the subject. While he was expressing an assessment of the show, Sir Elton gave his attention to Natalie.

'Have you known Miles long, my dear?'

'Only a few weeks.'

'So that's why I didn't see you at the hospital dance. The doctors are always expected to invite all the pretty women they know!'

'You're lucky in having two to bring,' Natalie smiled.

'Yes, I am, aren't I?' he said appreciatively, and gazed fondly from his wife to his daughter, who was still talking earnestly to Miles.

The buzzer sounded in the bar and people began

to move towards the auditorium.

'If you haven't committed yourselves to going anywhere special afterwards,' the older man asked, 'we would be delighted if you would join us for dinner.'

'We wouldn't dream of intruding,' Miles said hastily.

'Don't be silly, Miles,' Lady Hunter gushed. 'How on earth can you be intruding when you're one of the family?'

'In that case we would be delighted to join you,' Miles replied, though he looked anything but pleased as he escorted Natalie back to their seats. His obvious irritation made her feel surprisingly despondent and she wondered if he was annoyed because he had to be with Gayle after all, or because the time with herself was going to be prolonged.

Deciding it must be the latter reason, she said quietly: 'I'm sorry you'll be stuck with me after the theatre.'

He looked at her blankly, then suddenly smiled.

'I wasn't intending to rush you straight home,' he informed her dryly. 'At least not without feeding you first!'

'It wouldn't harm me to miss a meal.' She felt suddenly pleased he had not intended to shun her once Gayle was out of sight.

'Don't tell me you're one of those females who are everlastingly on a diet?'

She smiled. 'Not at all. I love my food too much for that!'

'So do I.'

She eyed him. 'I can't believe that.'

'It's true. But no matter how much I eat, I never put on an ounce.' He waited. 'Aren't you going to say it?'

'What?'

'That I burn it off with bad temper!'

'More likely you burn it off with your perfectionism. You are a perfectionist, aren't you, when it comes to your work?'

'How did you guess?'

'You're easy to read.' It was not the answer she wanted to give, but it was the only one she dared utter. He would laugh at her if she told him she intuitively knew exactly the kind of surgeon he was: a dedicated and kind one who would treat all his patients alike, whether they were rich or poor.

'What will happen if Sir Elton doesn't recommend you to take over from him?' she asked impetuously.

'It would be a blow to my prestige. I'd probably accept an offer from another hospital.'

'Then do you think it wise to antagonise Gayle?'

'I don't need to marry in order to further my career,' he said coldly.

'But she's very beautiful.'

'So are flamingoes, but I don't want one as a wife!'

The tartness of his tone prevented her from laughing, but as the lights in the auditorium lowered, she made a mental note of his comment to tell Maggie—when it was safe for her friend to hear the whole story.

Not unexpectedly Sir Elton had booked a table at the Savoy, and there was no difficulty in their being moved to a larger one that would accommodate his two extra guests.

'We're with the loveliest women in the room,' he said benignly to Miles when they were seated.

'That's a compliment we women can echo,' said Natalie, and heard him chuckle, though when he spoke, it was to Miles.

'This dear girl is as bright as she's lovely.'

He went on chatting and Natalie glanced surreptitiously at Lady Hunter, noticing the strength of character behind the chocolate-box prettiness, and the hardness that lay in the depths of eyes only slightly less blue than those of her daughter. Natalie then studied Gayle, who was gazing adoringly into Mile's face, giving no sign of being aware that he was with another girl.

'Do let's dance before we start eating,' said Gayle, and pulled Miles to his feet.

Reluctantly he followed her on to the floor, looking extremely tall in close proximity to the slender blonde beside him.

'What a lovely couple they make,' Lady Hunter sighed. 'Don't you think so, Elton?'

'You know I do, my dear.'

The woman gave Natalie a beady glance. 'Miles and Gayle have known each other since they were children. His mother and I always hoped....'

'I know,' Natalie said gently, 'Miles has told me.'

Lady Hunter looked startled and Natalie took advantage of it. She did not know exactly why she wanted to help Miles, only that she did, and that it had nothing whatever to do with her desire to save the Marriage Bureau.

'Miles has often spoken of you and Gayle and told me how fond he is of you all. He thinks of Gayle as another sister.'

'She doesn't see him as a brother.'

'What a pity,' said Natalie, and met the blue eyes defiantly.

'Let's order, shall we?' said Sir Elton. 'And perhaps our choice will inspire the other two when they come back to the table.'

Miles and Gayle returned in a surprisingly short

time, with Gayle's eyes flashing ominously in Natalie's direction. Whatever it was that Miles had said, she had obviously found it displeasing.

The dinner was perfect, and they were at the coffee stage when Miles asked his hostess to dance. Sir Elton chose this time to put in a call to the hospital, leaving Natalie and Gayle alone together.

'You won't get him, you know,' Gayle snapped, no longer bothering to make her voice dulcet. 'Miles is mine and I mean to have him.'

'Perhaps you'd better tell Miles so, before you tell me.'

'You're the one I'm concerned with,' Gayle snapped. 'I would hate you to go on wasting your time.'

'I don't think I am wasting it.'

Colour flooded into Gayle's face, giving an unpleasant redness to the peaches and cream skin. 'There's many a slip between cup and lip, Miss Baker, and you're nowhere near the cup yet.'

'Things have changed.' Natalie was beginning to feel sorry for Gayle. 'Just because a man doesn't say "no", it's unwise to think he means "yes". Miles doesn't love you. If he did, he wouldn't be seeing me.'

'Perhaps you're more accommodating than I am.'

It took a second for Natalie to understand what Gayle meant, then it was her turn to change colour, and she was still flushed when Miles returned to the table. He did not sit down, but put his hand on her shoulder and drew her on to the floor.

'It looks as if I just got back to the table in time,' he said calmly. 'We're you two fighting over me?'

'Oh, shut up,' she said crossly, and felt him miss a step.

'So you were,' he continued. 'What did Gayle say?'

'What marvellous weather we were having.'

His hold tightened. 'You're very lovely when you're in a temper, Natalie, but relax now. You're playing into Gayle's hands by getting annoyed.'

'There speaks someone who's played into her hands for years!'

Unwittingly so,' he said on a sigh, and suddenly twirled her round in an intricate step.

Taken by surprise, Natalie stumbled and his grip tightened. 'That was good,' he said, and proceeded again. 'Once more for luck,' he murmured, and twirled her round again.

He was an excellent dancer and moved with a precision that made him easy to follow. Gradually her tenseness evaporated and she lost herself in the music, aware only of the tempo changing from a quickstep to something slow and languorous which enabled him to relax his grip and draw her closer still. She was conscious of his height and thought involuntarily that it was a good thing operating tables were high, or he would get a terrible backache. She giggled and he lowered his head and looked into her face.

'What's the joke?'

'Nothing important.'

He didn't press the point, but rested his chin on her hair again. It was pleasant to feel the weight of it and the warmth of his breath which occasionally tickled her ear. Though he had urged her to relax, she sensed that he was still tense, and she glanced up at him and saw a nerve twitching at the side of his eyes. It made him look so vulnerable that she longed to comfort him.

'Gayle is a bitch,' she heard herself say softly, and wondered where the words had come from. But his reaction was equally astonishing, for he flung back his head and laughed loudly.

'Coming from you, that's a great admission,' he said, at last.

'Meaning I'm a bitch too?'

'Oh no,' he said instantly. 'Meaning that until now, you're tried to find reasons for me not to run away from her.'

'I merely said I found it ridiculous that you should *have* to run.'

'You wouldn't find it ridiculous if you knew my mother,' he told her. 'She's set her heart on having Gayle as a daughter-in-law, and I haven't wanted to hurt her by saying a firm "no". She has a bad heart,' he added, by way of explanation, 'and everyone in the family is careful not to upset her.'

'Don't you think it will upset her more if you let her go on believing something will happen when you know it won't?'

'Yes,' he admitted, pulling her closer. 'That's why being seen with you was such a good idea.'

'If you're seen any closer to me,' she said tartly, 'we'll merge together.'

'What a lovely idea!'

'Save the verbal flattery—no one can hear you.'

'What makes you think I don't mean it?'

'For a woman-hater you're a very fast worker, Mr Denton.'

'I didn't say I was a woman-hater,' he protested. 'Merely that I don't want to get married.'

'Then you're very safe,' she replied, 'because I don't either.'

She knew as she spoke that she was lying, and that she had only done so to protect herself. Did Miles Denton see her as someone with whom he could flirt and then discard, the way Gayle had suggested only a short time ago?

Working girls like herself were probably considered fair game by men in his social world. The very thought of this made her long to lash out at him, and she did so, not caring what she said.

'I'm only helping you because you blackmailed me into it. If I had a choice in the matter I would never go out with a man like you.'

His jaw clenched. 'What *am* I like?'

'Self-opinionated and arrogant. You're conceited too. You believe you only have to smile at a woman for her to fall for you. And yet you're so contemptuous of them. I dislike that more than anything.'

'I'm not contemptuous,' he said. 'I'm scared.'

For a moment she was too surprised to speak. Giving the matter thought, and taking his background into account, it was not as ludicrous as it seemed.

'Have you always been scared of women?' she asked.

'From the time I realised that they were attracted to me.'

'That must have been when you were five!'

He smiled. 'Fifteen, actually. The Matron at my school suddenly began to notice me—in the wrong way.'

'How awful!' Natalie was indignant. 'Didn't you tell your parents?'

'I was too ashamed.'

'So what did you do?'

'Made damn sure I was never ill! After that I concentrated on work, and in the hospital I got a reputation for being a misogynist. If I needed a girl to take to a dance I'd go with Gilly or Gayle—when they were old enough. That's how Gayle got the idea I was in love with her.'

Natalie was almost about to tell him that Gayle

didn't believe this for a minute, when she stopped, knowing he would not believe her. He saw Gayle as helpless and dumb, and it would be hard to convince him otherwise. Poor Miles, he might be a brilliant surgeon, but take the knife away from him and he was a singularly naïve man.

'Why are you smiling?' he demanded.

'I was thinking how silly you are, and that I'm rather pleased to be able to save you.'

'From a fate worse than death?'

The music stopped, but he was still chuckling at her remark as they returned to the table. Sir Elton and his wife were about to leave and Natalie saw that it was long past midnight.

'We'll see you tomorrow evening,' Lady Hunter said to Miles. 'Can you make it for dinner?'

'I'm afraid I can't,' he answered regretfully. 'I have several late appointments, but I'll be along shortly after nine.'

They moved out of the restaurant to the foyer.

'Can we expect you for the weekend?' the woman continued. 'My nephew and his wife are flying in from the States and——'

'I'm taking Natalie down to see my mother,' Miles intervened gently, and could not have created more of a furore if he had suddenly divested himself of his clothes. It was, Natalie thought, a master stroke on his part to have said he was introducing her to his mother, and she took back all thought of his being naïve.

'Another weekend, perhaps,' he continued smoothly, at the same time putting his hand on Natalie's arm so that she had to keep pace with him as they reached the entrance.

Silently she climbed ahead of him into their taxi, and they moved down the Strand.

'I thought that went off very well,' he said in the darkness. 'Sir Elton liked you.'

'I liked him.'

The taxi turned sharply down Kingsway and Natalie slid across the seat into Miles's arms. She went to pull away from him, but he would not let her go.

'I hope you don't mind my co-opting you for the weekend?' he said. 'But I think you'll enjoy it.'

'You meant it seriously?' She was surprised and pleased.

'Of course. I thought having my mother meet you was a stroke of genius. She'll prattle on about it all week, and if that doesn't convince Gayle and her mama that I'm serious about you, nothing will.'

Disappointed that this was the only reason for Miles's invitation, Natalie reverted to her earlier sarcasm.

'I hope you intend telling your mother the truth about us?'

'That's not possible. My mother's a darling but a very poor liar.'

'Unlike her son.'

'Don't you ever let up?' he remanded roughly, and pulled her closer.

She struggled to free herself, but he still would not let her go. Clasping her more firmly, he pushed her back against the side of the taxi so that it was impossible for her to move.

'You've been asking for this ever since we met,' he muttered in a low, throbbing voice, 'so lie still and enjoy it!'

Then he was kissing her, his lips firm but not hard

upon her own, his hands strong on her shoulders, but somehow comforting.

Determined not to demean herself by struggling with him, Natalie remained quiescent. But as the touch of his mouth became gentle, she involuntarily responded, and when his lips began to move softly across hers, she echoed the movement. Her body relaxed, and he was instantly aware of it and pulled her forward to cradle her more comfortably in his arms, his hands softly caressing her hair and the side of her face.

'You're beautiful,' he said huskily. 'Beautiful, and I want you.'

Again their lips met and hers parted beneath his. The momentary fear she had felt when he had first held her had gone completely, along with her antagonism.

The taxi slowed down and stopped and Miles lifted his mouth from hers and gave a little mutter. Hurriedly she smoothed her hair and then let him help her from the cab, while he paid off the man and then unlocked the door of his own car for her to climb in.

The streets were deserted and they reached her flat far more quickly than she would have liked.

'I won't ask you up for a drink,' she said, opening the car door.

'Pity,' he replied. 'I wouldn't have refused.' He reached across to shut her in with him. 'Why the rush, Natalie?'

'Because it's late and I'm sure you're operating early in the morning.'

'I wouldn't mind operating late at night as well!' he teased, and she chuckled, for it was the first openly humorous remark he had made to her. It was unbelievable that she and Miles should be joking together.

'I thought we'd leave town on Saturday about eleven,' he said. 'That would get us home in time for lunch.'

'You really do mean me to come?'

'I would love my mother to meet you,' he said quietly, and leaned nearer, as if to kiss her, but she drew back, unaccountably shy.

'It's late,' she said breathlessly, and fumbled at the lock to open the door.

He bent to do it for her, his face so close that she had only to purse her mouth to kiss his cheek, and the urge to do it was so strong that she was frightened.

I can't be feeling this way about him, she thought nervously. I hardly know him.

Quickly she stumbled from the car, and as she mounted the steps to her front door, found him beside her.

He took the key from her hand and opened the lock. She stepped into the hall and was illuminated by a moonbeam shining down through the fanlight. It turned her hair into a dark nimbus and silvered her dress.

'Even when all the colouring is taken away from you,' he said softly, 'you still seem to vibrate with it.'

Silently she stared at him, not knowing what to say.

'Seeing you and Gayle standing side by side,' he went on, 'made me look at her with different eyes.'

'And made you realise how beautiful she was,' Natalie replied coolly, finding her voice.

'How beautiful,' he agreed, 'and how empty. So different from you.' His hand came out and tilted up her chin. 'It's the nasty light in those gorgeous eyes of yours that I like. And the scorpion's tongue concealed by a Cupid's mouth.'

His head lowered and he spoke against her lips.

'Goodnight, Natalie. I'll pick you up here on Saturday.'

Abruptly he was gone. She waited until the sound of his car died away, then slowly climbed the stairs to her flat. What a long time it was until Saturday!

Later, as she lay in bed, she mulled over their evening together and tried not to think of the future. Loving a man like Miles could be a torment, for he was frighteningly self-sufficient one moment and astonishingly vulnerable the next. To admit to an awareness of his vulnerability frightened her, for it showed that the emotion he aroused in her was different from anything she had experienced before. She could cope with desire, but she did not know how to cope with her urge to protect this tall, bone-thin man who seemed so happy to work himself into the ground.

Unseeingly she stared into the darkness, trying to guess what the future held for her, and accepting the fact that if it did not hold mocking sherry gold eyes, then she wanted no part of it.

CHAPTER SEVEN

NATALIE half expected Miles to call her at some stage during the next two days to say he had called off the weekend. It would be easy for him to find an excuse to do so. All he had to do was to pretend one of his patients needed him in London

But by Saturday morning there was still no postponement, and she searched out a small case and started to pack. She was ready long before time and, with an uncertainty that was not part of her normal character, she went through her clothes to make sure she had taken the correct ones. If Mrs Denton was as formal as Lady Hunter, there might be a big house party, and she had no intention of letting Miles feel ashamed of her.

Eleven o'clock arrived with no sign of him. The calm she had deliberately cultivated was slowly ebbing, and in its place came the fear that he would not turn up.

By half past eleven she was absolutely sure this was the case, and when the bell finally rang at twelve she sprang across to the door and flung it open as if chased by the Demon King himself.

Miles looked over her shoulder, somewhat startled, as if expecting to see another person. Discomfited, she stepped aside to let him come in.

'Sorry to be late,' he said, 'but I was detained at the hospital.'

The reason was so obvious, she was annoyed for not having thought of it herself.

'I was beginning to think you'd changed your mind,' she blurted out, and was happy to see his astonishment.

'I nearly did,' he said. 'But only to suggest we went down last night instead. But unfortunately one of my patients had a relapse and I didn't feel I should leave town.'

'Do you now?' Natalie asked, even happier to know Miles had wanted to lengthen their stay in the country. 'If you want to call off the weekend, I'm quite happy to stay here.'

He looked around him. 'So would I be.'

There was a gleam in his eyes as he stepped towards her and she hastily backed away.

'I think we'd better go after all!'

He grinned and picked up her case. 'What a girl you are for changing your mind!'

'I'd rather be safe than sorry,' she quipped.

'How do you know you would be?'

It was precisely because she knew she wouldn't be sorry that she was scared to stay here alone with him. But to admit such a thing was dangerous, and ignoring his question she went ahead of him to the car.

The day was beautiful, with bright sunshine and a blue sky, but it would have been beautiful to Natalie had it been raining, and because she knew this she felt vulnerable.

'Why so quiet?' he asked, giving her a quick glance.

'I'm beginning to get cold feet. Is your mother as difficult and overbearing as you are?'

'That's my girl,' he teased. 'I've missed your knives in the last few days!'

'Why didn't you ring me, then?' she asked, and instantly regretted the question when she saw his surprise.

'I wanted to, but I deliberately didn't. I have an idea you're the sort of girl who doesn't like to be chased.'

'Usually I don't, but I wasn't sure if you wanted to go ahead with this plan. I know you think it will convince Gayle, but I'm not so sure. She's so confident of roping you in eventually that I think she's willing to give you plenty of room to run wild!'

'My taking you home has nothing to do with Gayle,' he said, ignoring her other comment. 'When I first made the suggestion it did, but when I thought it over I realised it was what I *wanted* to do.' He slowed the car so that he could look at her. 'I hope you want it too, Natalie?'

'Very much,' she said in a trembling voice, and hastily averted her gaze. But she heard his soft laugh and there was no escaping the pressure of his fingers as his left hand reached out and clasped hers on her lap.

At one-thirty they reached Three Lawns, and bowling down the long drive towards the gracious house set in spacious terraced gardens, it was easy to see how it had earned its name.

Natalie looked at the tall spare frame behind the wheel of the car and wondered why Miles had made no concession to the fact that they were spending the weekend in the country. He was still wearing a formal grey suit and tie.

'Don't you ever relax completely?' she asked impetuously.

'I'm relaxed now.'

'I meant in jeans and sweater.'

'I'm not the jeans type. I find them damned uncomfortable to wear. But I promise you'll see me in baggy pants!'

His smile was swift and softened his austere features,

giving them a puckish, whimsical look.

'What do you think of the house?' he continued, as they came to a stop on a wide circular patch of gravel.

Directly facing her, Natalie saw a flight of shallow steps leading up to a narrow front door lying between two graceful windows. The house was smaller than she had anticipated from her first glimpse of it, and built of mellow stone some hundred years ago. It looked as serene and gracious as the tall, grey-haired woman who had opened the door and was coming forward to meet them. There was no guessing required to know it was Miles's mother, for she had the same slender figure and sherry brown eyes as her two children.

Natalie found the eyes looking at her intently as they smiled a welcome, and her hand was taken in a firm but cool grasp. Mrs Denton chatted gently in a well-modulated voice as she ushered her guest through the small, square hall and up the elegant sweeping staircase. Within a few moments Natalie found herself in a bedroom that overlooked the back of the house and the peaceful gardens beyond.

'I hope you'll be comfortable here,' Mrs Denton was saying. 'If there's anything you need, do let me know.'

'It looks as if I'll have everything,' Natalie replied, looking at the bedside table which held a supply of paperbacks, a couple of fashion magazines and a small pottery jar filled with digestive biscuits.

'Just in case you're hungry in the night,' her hostess informed her, adding: 'Once, when my husband was alive, we stayed with some dear friends who both had appetites like birds. We were practically starving for the entire three days we were there, and after that I vowed I would never let the same thing happen to my own guests!'

'If I'm hungry I promise to tell you,' Natalie laughed, and Mrs Denton left her alone to unpack her case, telling her to come down as soon as she was ready.

Deciding it was not necessary to change for lunch, Natalie paused only to comb her hair before going downstairs and out into the garden. It was even lovelier than it had appeared from a distance, for everywhere the scent of flowers wafted up to her and there was no sound in the air except the occasional drone of an aircraft and the buzzing of a bee.

The lawn nearest the house was well tended, but on the second one, which was on a lower level, bushes were allowed to grow haphazardly, giving an unexpected impression of size to what was a relatively small area. The third section of the garden was by far the largest, and also the wildest, as was the one Natalie appreciated most. Here there was a profusion of roses—her favourite flower—in a brilliant mass of scented colours, as well as flowering shrubs of every description and age. Narrow paths wandered haphazardly, going nowhere in particular, and she strolled down one and found herself in front of a small pergola covered with pink climbing roses. Delightedly she touched a cluster of blooms, admiring the varying shades of pink.

'You like roses?' Miles asked, and she swung round and saw he was standing a few feet away from her.

As he had promised, he had changed into baggy pants, but they did nothing to disguise his tall thinness. Yet the half-buttoned shirt he was wearing disclosed a ripple of muscles across his chest and gave an impression of wiry strength. As a surgeon, she knew, he would have to be in the peak of condition. Standing operating for hours at a stretch required the highest physical stamina. But he should learn not to abuse it; should not work such long hours and have so little recreation.

She wondered if Gayle was aware of this, but could not see the blonde girl caring for anyone's wellbeing other than her own. Aware of Miles watching her, Natalie realised she had not yet answered his question.

'Roses are my favourite flower,' she said.

'You remind me of a rose yourself.'

She straightened. 'Full-blown and gaudy?'

His chuckle was appreciative. 'Rich and heady is the way I would have put it.' His thin fingers were cool on her chin as they tilted her head to face him.

'If I didn't know you to be a liberated, quick-tempered firebrand, I would say that today you are almost shy of me.'

'Quick-tempered firebrands can still be capable of shyness.'

'Surely not after all this time?'

'All this time?' she countered. 'We hardly know each other!'

She saw his eyes narrow for an instant. 'You're right,' he said slowly, 'yet I feel as if I've known you for a long time. Maybe it's because I feel at home with you.'

'I'm a real home-body,' she mocked.

'It's a body I would very much like to be at home with,' he replied, his sherry gold eyes appraising her curves.

She blushed and pulled back from him. Miles Denton was a surprising man; he looked ascetic as a saint yet he kissed with the fire of Satan.

'Come on,' she said brightly. 'Show me the rest of the garden.'

He led her through a tangle of tall grass to where a stream marked the southern boundary, and they looked across to the rolling green fields beyond.

'Aren't you afraid it might be built on?' she asked, pointing to the sweep of land.

'That's a farm,' he replied, 'and I own it.'

She was surprised. 'I don't see you as a farmer.'

'Nor do I,' he smiled. 'Hence the fact that it's tenanted. But there is a beautiful farmhouse that I plan to occupy one day.'

'When the farmer and his wife move out?'

'That was part of the agreement. But they'll have another place to go to.'

Natalie knew without asking that he planned to live in the farmhouse either when he married or when he retired. As he had said he did not wish to change his happy single status, she assumed that retirement would come first—unless Gayle won the day. Natalie tried to push the thought out of her mind.

'Would you like to see the farmhouse?' Miles asked.

'We don't have time now,' said Natalie, strangely reluctant to say yes. 'Your mother said lunch would be served soon.'

'Then we'd better go back. We can go to the farm another time.'

Wishing she had not refused the offer after all, she turned and followed him back to the house, reaching the top lawn as Mrs Denton came out through the french windows, a small gong in her hands.

'You've saved me calling you,' she announced, and beckoned them inside.

'It's such a lovely day I thought we would have had lunch on the terrace,' Miles commented, as they took their places round the beautifully polished Sheraton table.

'Mrs Dorcas had already laid it in here and I hate giving her extra work,' his mother said. 'But we'll have it on the terrace tomorrow if the weather still holds. I assume you won't have to rush away?'

'Not unless there's an emergency.'

'Don't you ever get a complete weekend to yourself?' Natalie asked.

'I'm free now,' he smiled. 'One of my colleagues is standing in for me, and he's very capable.'

'But you said that if there were an emergency you would have to go.'

'It isn't a question of having to, Natalie, it's a question of wanting to do so. If anything serious cropped up with one of my patients I would expect my colleague to let me know. Then it would be my decision whether or not I wished to return.'

'And of course you would,' his mother stated.

'Of course,' he said, as if it were the most natural thing in the world.

Natalie's eyes met those of her hostess and the two women smiled, as if sharing a secret.

You see how dedicated he is, the older woman seemed to be saying. It isn't just a job to him, he really cares.

Yet it was not only about his patients that Miles cared, Natalie knew, but also about the people in his life—his mother, with whom he obviously had a good relationship, and his sister. What a fool Gillian was not to realise he had her best interests at heart. She should be glad she had a brother who worried about her, and not go out of her way to defy him. Yet if Gillian had not done so, Miles would not now be in her own life.

Lunch over, they returned to the garden. Mrs Denton took a sewing basket and was soon absorbed in some tapestry. Natalie leafed through a magazine and Miles promptly fell asleep in a chaise-longue, his arms against his sides, long, supple hands dangling.

'He works so hard,' Mrs Denton said quietly, looking at him. 'I'm always glad when he can get down for a weekend. I feel it's the only time he has to himself.'

'But he loves his work,' said Natalie, and wondered whether her hostess wished that Gayle was sharing her son's weekend. But Mrs Denton's next words were a denial of this.

'It's lovely having you here, Natalie. You're the first girl Miles has brought here to see me. He usually keeps his private life very private.'

Natalie wished she were not here under false pretences. 'I haven't known Miles very long,' she said carefully.

'But long enough for him to bring you to meet me.'

'I don't think meeting a man's mother means as much these days as it did years ago.'

'It means a lot to Miles. If it didn't, he'd have brought other girl's home.'

'You're embarrassing Natalie, Mother.' Miles suddenly spoke, his voice clipped, surprising both women. 'If you aren't careful, she'll turn tail and run back to London.'

'No, I won't,' Natalie replied stoutly. 'You promised me a country weekend and a country weekend I'm going to have.'

'I thought you were sleeping,' Mrs Denton said to him, 'not eavesdropping.'

'It was not intentional, Mamma,' her son smiled, 'merely the habit of years. I've become used to sleeping with one ear alert for the telephone to ring.'

'Well, no telephone bell will waken you this afternoon, so go to sleep again.'

'Only if you promise not to talk about me.'

'I'm sure your mother and I can think of more amusing subjects than you,' Natalie rejoined.

'I don't believe it,' he replied, and closing his eyes again, was almost instantly asleep.

'Men can do that,' Mrs Denton said, looking at him fondly. 'I've even known him to do it when we've been in the middle of a quarrel.'

Natalie chuckled. 'How infuriating!'

'It is rather,' Mrs Denton smiled back. 'Not that I quarrel with him very often. He's a wonderful son. Our only disharmony is because he's still a bachelor. I've been wanting him to marry for years.'

Not anxious to be the recipient of her hostess's confidences, Natalie rose from her deck chair and pretended an interest in an unusual-looking bush a few yards away. Mrs Denton was a keen gardener and was soon happily absorbed in telling her about a rare species of lavender, and then going on to show various other kinds. By the time Natalie had learned everything she wanted to know about lavender bushes, a servant was wheeling a trolley on to the lawn. Homemade scones surrounded a delicious-looking fruit cake whose sweet aroma roused Miles from his sleep, and made him sit up and announce that he was famished.

'After your enormous lunch!' Natalie exclaimed. 'I can't see where you're going to put any more food.'

'I've got hollow legs,' he said, proffering her a scone and demolishing one himself. 'Anyway, my nervous energy consumes all the calories I eat.'

'I thought it was your bad temper that did that,' she said sweetly.

'I'm only bad-tempered with you,' he rejoined with a glint in his eyes. 'Normally I'm the most docile of men.'

Thinking of the way he had allowed Gayle to play havoc with his life, she was almost ready to believe him, but it was an unpalatable thought that Miles's ambition was strong enough to allow him to be forced to the brink of a marriage he did not want, and not for the first time Natalie wondered how he had planned to get out of the situation had she herself not come on the scene.

'What are you thinking about?' Miles asked softly, and Natalie saw that Mrs Denton had moved out of earshot to fondle a red setter that had ambled on to the lawn.

'About you and Gayle,' Natalie said truthfully. 'I wonder if you'll really manage to escape from her clutches.'

'It might be a question of going from the frying pan into the fire.'

'What do you mean?'

He gave her an odd look. 'At least I find Gayle easy to understand and not that difficult to manage; whereas another woman might be considerably more difficult to tame. You, for example, could very well turn round and bite the hand that's feeding you!'

'Since I consider I would be providing part of the food,' Natalie retorted, 'I would bite any hand that thought it was feeding me entirely!'

'Oh, lord,' he groaned. 'A woman who wants to stand on her own feet! I should have known you wouldn't see marriage as enough to keep you happy.'

'Would you?'

'Would I what?'

'Would you stop being a surgeon if you had a wife?' Before he could answer she went on: 'Then why should you expect the woman you marry to give up her career?'

'Because I consider that taking care of a home and children is a full-time career in itself. At least until the children are old enough to take care of themselves.'

'By which time the woman feels too old to go back to her job, or discovers that her knowledge is so out of date that she's got to retrain.'

'I grant you it's a problem,' he said, 'but it's one that a woman has to face. And one day you'll have to face it too. Unless you plan to marry a man who'll stay home and let *you* go to work!'

Before she could open her mouth to protest, he reached across and put his fingers upon her lips.

'We're having an unnecessary argument, Natalie. You have a job that will turn you into an ideal wife. If you're used to caring for other people's toddlers, you can easily look after half a dozen of your own.'

For a second, indignation flashed from her eyes, but then the humour of his remark got the better of her temper, and as he felt her lips twitch beneath his touch, he dropped his fingers away from them.

'You see,' he continued smoothly, 'you have everything to recommend you.'

'I'll get you to write out a reference,' she said promptly.

'I must make a few other tests first.'

The gleam in his eyes warned her not to ask what he meant, and instead she helped herself to another scone.

After tea they went for a walk across to the farmhouse, which was every bit as beautiful as she had anticipated. They did not go into it but admired its timbered grace from a distance before returning across the fields to Three Lawns. Miles left her at the door of her room and then went to his own further down the corridor.

'Do we get dressed for dinner?' she called softly.

'Only into something comfortable,' he answered.

Surveying the clothes she had with her, Natalie was glad she had brought a good selection. How awful to have gone down in chiffon and found Miles and his mother in cashmere and slacks.

Deliberately she chose a loose flowing silk that relied for its result on the curves of the figure which it covered. The wild rose colour emphasised the flush in her cheeks and gave unexpected depth to her Titian hair.

When she entered the sitting room Miles and his mother were already there. He was unexpectedly suave in narrow fitting black suede pants and a brown velvet jacket almost the same colour as his eyes. So he could become the man about town when it suited him! It was an interesting thought and she wondered what other possibilities lay behind his usually austere façade.

Yet today he had not been austere with her, but charming and friendly with a hint of something deeper behind it. Yet she knew enough not to read too much into his friendliness, no matter that he had said he had asked her home because he had wanted to do so.

With an effort she focused her attention on what Mrs Denton was saying, but found it hard to prevent her attention from wandering as Miles came over with a brimming glass. The rim was frosted, and she looked at it in astonishment.

'What is it?' she asked. 'Sugar?'

'Salt.' Seeing she did not believe him, he smiled. 'It really is salt, Natalie. It goes with this particular drink.'

'You mean I sip it and get a mouthful of salt at the

same time?' She still did not believe him.

'Hardly a mouthful, just a slight taste. There's only a faint powdering of salt round the edge of the glass.'

Doubtfully she took it and sipped, finding it perfectly delicious. 'What is it?' she asked.

'It's called a Marguerita. I was first given it when I was in Mexico. It's a mixture of tequila, dry sack and a little fresh lime.'

'I could develop a taste for this,' she said.

Miles chuckled, as did his mother who, in a floral silk dress with a long flowing skirt, looked considerably younger and very much like her daughter Gillian.

When Natalie had finished her drink they moved across to the dining room. Dinner was a predominantly cold meal, with only a hot soup served as a first course. But the food was ample and deliciously cooked: fresh salmon washed down by a fairly dry Chablis, and a delicious iced almond gâteau accompanied by a Barsac, the first truly sweet wine Natalie could ever remember having tasted.

'I can see you have a sweet tooth,' Miles commented, watching her look of appreciation as she sipped from the small glass.

'I didn't think I had,' she confessed, 'but I must say I find this wine absolutely marvellous.'

'Go easy on it,' Mrs Denton cautioned. 'I once made the mistake of thinking it was non-alcoholic because it was so sweet.'

Natalie, who had drunk her glass rather quickly, was beginning to be aware of the effect. She shook her head when Miles wanted to replenish her glass, but he ignored the gesture.

'I shall get drunk,' she protested.

'The thought had occurred to me,' he said carefully,

'and it might be interesting to see what you do.'

'Something disgraceful, I should think!'

'If you did, it wouldn't go further than these four walls,' he said solemnly, though his eyes were glowing gold, which she knew to be a sign that he was in a high good humour.

'Do you remember when Gayle had too much to drink?' Mrs Denton said suddenly.

Her words acted like a douche of cold water upon Natalie's spirits, reminding her once again that she would be wise not to forget she was here for a specific purpose.

'I certainly do remember,' Miles answered his mother. 'She got frightfully peevish too.' He glanced at Natalie. 'I think *in vino veritas* is a remarkably true saying, don't you?'

'As I don't know how I behave when I'm drunk, I'm going to let that pass without comment,' Natalie smiled.

'Well, I can't imagine *you* being peevish. Downright bad-tempered is much more your line!'

'Miles!' his mother expostulated. 'How can you be so rude?'

'Miles and I have a particularly truthful relationship,' Natalie said quickly, wishing it were not quite the case. 'When we first met, we decided we would never lie to one another.'

'How did you meet?' asked Mrs Denton with interest.

Natalie was at a loss how to answer, but Miles had no hesitation.

'Through Gillie,' he said, setting down his empty wine glass and touching his napkin to his mouth.

'I didn't realise you were a friend of Gillie's,' Mrs Denton said to Natalie.

'Not really a friend,' Natalie replied. 'More of an acquaintance.'

Anxious to change the subject, she said the first thing that came into her head. 'I love the decor of this room. Did you do it, or was it like this when you moved in?'

'It was almost a shell when my husband and I bought it,' Mrs Denton replied. 'We spent the best part of ten years lovingly re-doing every room, and the year after we finished it, my husband died.'

Natalie looked sympathetic but said nothing, feeling that any words she uttered would be inadequate.

'It was very sudden,' Mrs Denton went on. 'One minute he was sitting in his armchair talking to me, and the next minute he was gone. It was a dreadful shock.' Her lips trembled and for a moment there was silence. 'But Miles and Gillie were wonderful to me,' the woman continued, 'and now I can think of it without too much pain.' She leaned back in her chair, a slim, regal figure. 'My husband was considerably older than I am. He was forty when he married. That's why I don't want Miles to wait too long. I think one should grow up with one's children.'

'I agree,' Natalie said, 'but one can't get married until the right person comes along.'

'If you go round with your eyes closed, how will you find them?'

'I don't go around with my eyes closed,' Miles protested. 'After all, I found Natalie.'

Natalie flung him a look of reproach, wishing he were not pretending quite so well in front of his mother. She liked Mrs Denton considerably—a fact which did nothing to lessen the guilt she felt.

'I don't want to wait until I'm seventy before I see

some grandchildren,' Mrs Denton continued. 'It's time we had children playing on the lawn again.'

'If you're asking me to confess my sins and bring them home,' her son teased, 'I'm perfectly willing to do so.'

'Miles! You know very well that isn't what I meant.'

'I know what you mean, Mamma dear, but you won't make me change my mind by nagging at me. Leave your little chickens alone and they'll come home to roost all in good time.'

Natalie felt Mrs Denton's eyes upon her and though she pretended to be unaware of it, she felt the colour in her cheeks intensify.

Luckily Mrs Dorcas chose that moment to come in with the coffee, and Miles wandered over to the stereo to put on some music.

'Ever since he was a child, music has helped him to relax,' Mrs Denton confided, glancing at the tall thin figure of her son intently scanning through some cassettes. 'He's an excellent violinist. At one time we thought he was going to take it up professionally, but then surgery took precedence.' She half smiled. 'Not surprising, really, when one considers how well known James was in his profession.'

'I hadn't realised Miles's father was a surgeon too,' Natalie commented, and wished Miles had told her.

One of the Brandenburg Concertos filled the room with sound, and listening to the clear notes she decided how much like Miles Bach's music was, being full of controlled passion and with a depth of feeling one could only appreciate the more one listened to it.

Miles sat in an armchair, body totally relaxed, one hand moving in time with the tempo. The Bach was followed by Mahler's Eighth Symphony, and during the last part Mrs Denton stood up, mouthed 'Goodnight' and left the room.

Miles rose and silently went with her to the door, then returned to sit beside Natalie on the settee. His long legs made a dark line a bare three inches from her rose-coloured skirts.

He gave no sign of being aware of her but she knew he had not come to sit beside her merely because it was more comfortable, and she was not surprised when, a moment later, his hand came out and clasped hers. There was a tremor in his touch she had not anticipated, and she would have given a great deal to have known whether it was from nervousness or desire.

The music came to an end and neither of them moved.

'You look even lovelier than usual tonight, Natalie,' he said softly, and drew her gently into his arms.

She did not resist him but remained passive as he tilted up her chin with one hand and looked into her eyes.

'I'm not forcing myself upon you this time,' he continued. 'If you don't want me to kiss you, all you have to do is to say no.'

Silently she continued to stare into his eyes, and the glow in them deepened as passion arose in him. Moving slowly, as if he had all the time in the world, his mouth came down upon hers and he pushed her gently lower on to the settee. Her thick silky hair splayed out around her and he wound his fingers through it as he went on kissing her.

His touch seared through her like a flame and she wrapped her arms around him, forgetting she had wanted to play this scene coolly. All she was aware of was the need to respond to him—to try to assuage the clamorous urge that his kisses aroused in her body. His hands moved upon her breasts and she felt the pressure of them through the silky folds of her dress.

'So much material,' he whispered with wry humour. 'Did you wear it by design or accident?'

'A designing accident!'

He chuckled and, half raising her, skilfully went to lower the zip. But the very proficiency of his movements caused her to pull away from him.

'For someone who professes to have limited experience with women,' she said shakily, 'you're very adept at undressing them.'

'As a medical student I often had to do so.'

'Instead of the nurses?'

'They weren't always available.' His hands remained on her shoulders. 'Though I said my experience was limited, I can't remember saying *how* limited!'

'It isn't even a word you should use,' she said. 'I think you're an experienced, artful man, Miles Denton.'

'Obviously not artful enough.' He cupped her breasts again and then let them go and put his hands on her back, pressing her body tightly against his own. He was trembling noticeably. 'If I said I didn't normally behave like this, you wouldn't believe me.'

'How right you are!'

'Nevertheless it happens to be true. You tantalise me. It must be that wine-red hair of yours, making me drunk.'

It was one of the prettiest compliments ever paid to the colour of her hair, and she clung to him and tilted her face up—a gesture which he read correctly, for he stopped speaking and started to kiss her again. Then, still keeping his mouth pressed to hers, he drew her down on to the settee once more. He made no attempt to lower her dress, and though she was sorry, she was nonetheless glad. Even his kisses aroused her to a desire she had rarely felt before, and the fear she had experienced with him deepened, for she knew she was no longer tottering on the brink of falling in love with him; she had already done so.

Her lips parted and Miles gently moved the tip of his tongue along the inner edge of them. She knew he would do no more unless she encouraged him, and her own need out-weighed her caution. Gently, she too traced his lips with her tongue, and feeling the moist sweetness of her, he deepened his kiss, with sensuous movements that sent desire storming through her.

'Darling,' he said hoarsely, and then with a convulsive shiver pushed her away from him and stood up. He strode over to the mantelpiece and rested his clenched hands upon the marble top.

'I'm not as much in control as I thought,' he muttered.

'Nor am I,' Natalie confessed. 'It might be better if we said goodnight.'

'No. I don't want you to go yet.' He glanced at her over his shoulder. 'I'll sit on the far side of the room. It's too early for you to go to bed. I want to go on looking at you.'

Once again he was proving himself no mean giver of compliments, so she rested her head against the brocade settee and watched as he settled into an armchair several yards away, with the easy co-ordination that was so much a part of him.

'You haven't put on another cassette,' she reminded him.

He looked surprised, then rose to do so, this time

choosing Max Bruch's Violin Concerto, a particular favourite of Natalie's. She had to restrain her desire to hum along with the music, until she was suddenly aware of a droning sound and realised that Miles himself was humming the tune, or at least what passed for it.

'What a dreadful voice you've got!' she laughed, delighted to find something he did not do well. He gave her an impish grin and went on singing.

'I'm glad you didn't take up music professionally,' she laughed when the concerto came to an end.

'I have perfect pitch,' he said mildly. 'It's just unfortunate that although I know the sound, it doesn't come out the way I hear it. Put me in front of an instrument and I'm fine.'

'Do you have a violin now?'

'Yes, but I'm not going to play tonight. I'm tired.' He hesitated. 'I'll play for you another night if you like.'

She saw he meant it and was touched, the more so since his comment signified that there would be other nights when they would be alone together. If only she could believe that his wanting to be with her had nothing to do with Gayle! She longed to ask him, yet dared not, and instead murmured that it was late and that she was going to bed.

'Care for a nightcap?' he asked.

'No more to drink,' she said, and left him standing by the decanter.

She was still at the dressing table brushing her hair, when she heard his step in the corridor. It did not hesitate outside her room, though there was a slight difference in the sound, as if he were quickening his pace rather than slowing it, and her lips curved in a smile. She went on with her brushing, not pausing until she had reached the hundredth stroke.

'Miles Denton.' She said the name aloud. How well the name suited him—firm yet unadorned. 'Miles Denton. Mrs Miles Denton.'

She put down her hairbrush and met her eyes in the mirror. They were bright as stars.

'Don't make a fool of yourself,' she warned her image. 'This is the 1980s, not the 1880s. A few kisses don't mean anything. Miles doesn't want to get married—he's already made that clear—but he's ripe for a love affair and all you need do is say yes.'

But when the affair was over, what then?

The answer to her question was a sobering one, and contemplating how bleak her future would be without Miles in it, she knew she had left it too late to run away.

CHAPTER EIGHT

SEVERAL of Mrs Denton's friends dropped in for pre-lunch drinks on Sunday, and it was mid-afternoon before lunch was finished.

Earlier, Miles had taken the retriever for a long walk across the fields while Natalie, not feeling energetic, had elected to stay behind with her hostess. She found herself liking the woman more and more and inevitably feeling guiltier than ever for being here under false pretences.

She thought of this now as she watched Miles sleeping in a deck chair, his face dappled by the late afternoon sunshine.

'He never takes a holiday long enough to relax,' Mrs Denton said, seeing Natalie's eyes resting on her son's face. 'It's so bad for him. That's why I'd like him to get married. If he had someone else's well-being to care about, he'd take more care of himself.'

'He cares deeply about his patients.'

'Not in the same way that he would about his wife. I always hoped he and Gayle....' Mrs Denton sighed. 'I'm sorry, my dear. It's not very tactful of me to have said that to you.'

'It doesn't matter. Miles told me you and Lady Hunter have always hoped they would fall in love with each other.'

'Gayle would marry Miles today, if he asked her.'

'Perhaps if you didn't push her at him, he might not be so obstinate,' Natalie said evenly, marvelling at her composure.

'It's very forbearing of you to say such a thing,' Mrs Denton murmured. 'You and Miles are obviously fond of each other.' There was a pause. 'Are you in love with him?'

Colour flooded Natalie's face and she glanced at Miles, thankful that he was asleep. But her calmness vanished as she saw one eyelid half lift and then swiftly close again. What a beast he was; he had been awake the whole time.

'Miles and I are only friends,' she said firmly, ignoring his shuttered face. 'The only thing serious about us is our intention *not* to get married.'

'But you seem so compatible,' Mrs Denton said. 'From the moment I saw you together I had the feeling you were important to him.'

Natalie's interest was aroused, and she gazed intently at her hostess, willing her to go on. It would at least give the Great Pretender something to think about.

'Miles is so considerate with you,' Mrs Denton continued, 'and he isn't by nature a considerate man. He's an extremely kind one and he'll do anything for anybody, but little gestures of thoughtfulness are not in his character. At least I didn't think so until I saw him with you.'

'I haven't found him particularly thoughtful,' Natalie said sweetly.

'That's because you don't know what he's usually like,' Mrs Denton chuckled. 'But he seems to be on pins and needles whenever you're out of the room and his eyes follow you around the whole time.' The older woman hesitated, her expression thoughtful. 'I've wanted Gayle for a daughter-in-law for as long as I can remember, yet now, meeting you, I find you are so much more restful. It's odd really, but I feel as if I've known you for years. Maybe it's because I know how much you like my son.'

This was coming too close to home and Natalie glanced across at Miles, who was still keeping his eyes closed, though she was prepared to bet a cent to a dollar that he was wide awake.

'I've never given a thought to marriage,' she said brightly. 'I warned Miles you might get the wrong idea if I came down for the weekend.'

'I always seem to be getting the wrong idea,' Mrs Denton said regretfully, and looked towards her son. Suddenly she seemed to notice that his lids were flickering and she smiled conspiratorially at Natalie, indicating that she should look at the recumbent figure.

Natalie glanced at Miles and found herself grinning as her hostess, having discovered her son was foxing, now seemed to take it for granted that every answer Natalie had given to her questions had been deliberately worded to tease Miles.

Rising, Mrs Denton tiptoed away, and Natalie settled herself more comfortably in her chair and waited for Miles to realise they were alone together.

'I think your son is far too selfish and bad-tempered to make a good husband,' she said conversationally. 'I don't expect you to answer me, Mrs Denton, because you're biased in his favour. But quite honestly, I think he deserves Gayle as a wife. She's exactly the snobby little horror he needs!'

Miles sat up in one sweeping movement, his whole expression one of indignation. In an instant he saw that he and Natalie were alone, and he gave a loud shout of laughter.

'My God, you're a bitch! For a moment you fooled me completely.' He stood up and stretched. 'I must say I expected to hear far more pleasant things about myself.'

'You know what they say about eavesdroppers,' Natalie replied. 'Anyway, it's cruel to let your mother think we're serious about each other.'

'It isn't cruel to let her know I like you.' Sherry gold eyes glittered at her. 'You knew I was only pretending to be asleep, so I discount everything you said. If you hadn't known I was awake, you would have answered her quite differently.'

'Oh, sure,' Natalie said calmly. 'I'd have told her I adore you madly and that my one ambition in life is to be your doormat.'

'Not a very soft one,' he said, straight-faced. 'But full of sharp prickles. Still, I'd soon soften them.'

'The one thing you aren't short of is conceit!'

'Because I know my worth?' Lithely he stretched his muscles again. 'Don't you think I have the makings of an excellent husband?'

'If you were on our books, I'd get you settled in no time.'

'I *am* on your books,' he reminded her, 'and I have a feeling that in next to no time you *will* get me settled.' He leaned forward and dropped a light kiss on the top of her head. 'Come, my sweet, we must be getting back. I have a few patients to see at the nursing home before they settle down for the night.'

'You were supposed to have the weekend completely free.'

'If I stayed here another night with you I might never be free again.'

The twitch of his mouth showed he was teasing, and wishing he weren't, Natalie went in to do her packing.

Her farewell to Mrs Denton was affectionate, and all

too soon they were speeding towards London. Miles seemed preoccupied, and Natalie wondered if he was thinking of his patients or about the weekend they had just spent together—well, not quite together. She fell to musing on what it might have been like had they really been alone; and experienced such an uprush of desire that she was shocked. So much for her independence of mind and body, she thought despairingly, when a teasing man—who made it clear he did not want marriage—could bring her to this state in a matter of days.

It was seven o'clock when Miles drew the car to a stop outside her apartment block, and she jumped out almost before he had switched off the engine.

'Thanks for a wonderful weekend, Miles.'

'What's the rush?' he demanded, getting out of the car and coming round towards her. 'The weekend isn't over yet. I'll be free again in about an hour and we can go out for supper.'

Because the urge to say yes was strong, she forced herself to say no.

'I'm tired,' she lied, 'and I have some things to prepare for tomorrow. I have to arrange interviews for two new clients and I must study their files.'

'You aren't going back to the office tonight, are you?'

'I brought them home with me.'

'How efficient you are!'

'I try to be,' she said lightly, and on an impulse put her hands on his arm. 'You do believe that Maggie and I didn't know anything about Roland contacting your sister? She doesn't realise the sort of person he is, but even if he were the greatest catch in the world she'd never do anything so unethical as to allow him to meet a client.'

'I believe you,' Miles said quietly, 'and right now I feel surprisingly magnanimous towards Roland. But for him, I'd never have met you.' He put his hands over hers and went to draw her close.

She stiffened and held herself away from him. She did not want him to consider her too easy.

'At least if you believe I knew nothing of what Roland was doing,' she whispered, 'I won't feel our friendship is——' She stopped, not wishing to give herself away.

'Let's pretend we met for the first time this weekend,' said Miles, and lowering his head, gently touched his mouth to hers. 'Are you free to see me on Tuesday night?' he asked.

Wishing only that he had made it Monday, she nodded.

'Then I'll pick you up here about eight,' he said. 'But bear with me if I'm not on time. I never know to the exact half hour.'

Happily she bade him goodnight. She wanted to relive every moment of the last two days and, as she unpacked her case and changed into a comfortable housecoat, she chewed over each incident like a dog on a bone, savouring every single bit of it.

Natalie's mood of happiness carried over into the next day, and she was singing cheerfully under her breath as she unlocked the door of the Bond Street office and picked up the pile of circulars and letters which lay on the mat. The circulars she dumped into the waste paper basket, and after reading the letters she put them into her handbag to show Maggie when she visited her that evening. How delighted her friend would be to hear from two clients who had sent wedding invitations and glowing thanks to Maggie for introducing them to their partners.

Natalie wondered if one day she would be able to say something similar to her friend, and laughed out loud at the idea. But after all, she had met Miles through the Whitney Marriage Bureau, so it would not be too far-fetched if one day she and Miles were to tell their children that this was the way their parents had found each other.

Don't think of marriage until you've received a proposal, she chided herself, yet could not stop her errant thoughts. Regardless of what he said, Miles was not the sort of man to put any other proposal to her; it would be marriage or nothing.

The thought that it might well be nothing was a disconcerting one, but she forced herself to acknowledge it. Despite his mother's hopes, Miles had organised his private life very well. He had a beautiful home, an obviously devoted secretary, and no doubt countless minions to do his bidding. What need did he have for a wife? Remembering the controlled passion with which he had kissed her, she thought jealously of the other girls he knew. Though he was too wary of Gayle to make love to her, it was a certainty that he did not go to bed alone every night.

With an effort she concentrated on the folders in front of her, and was delighted when the entry of a client forced her to concentrate on someone else's problems rather than her own. It was a Mr Calthorpe, who had already been introduced to five women without finding any of them to his liking.

'I merely came in to tell you that my firm is moving me to Paris for six months,' he said, 'and I wondered how this is going to affect me with you.'

Trying to guess what Maggie would do in the circumstances, Natalie suggested that his file be kept in abeyance until he informed them he was available for introductions again in London.

'I'll contact you when I get back,' he assured her, and gave her an admiring look. 'Someone like you would suit me fine.'

Promising to see if they had any redheads who met with his requirements, she bade him goodbye, then put his file away. There was another folder in the 'abeyance' section, and she glanced at it. It belonged to a man who, after paying his introductory fee, had suddenly found himself sent off to Africa for two years. Natalie saw that Maggie had immediately offered to refund his money, but he had refused to accept it, saying that since Miss Whitney had already introduced him to several nice women, one of whom had promised to write to him, he felt that having paid his fee had helped to change his luck.

Maybe the Whitney Marriage Bureau had changed her luck too, Natalie thought, and wondered what Miles was doing at this moment. Was he operating or was he going round the wards, pouring his charm upon his patients? How many of them were women, and were some of them young and beautiful? She could imagine many of them falling in love with him and donning their prettiest nightdresses when they knew he was coming to see them.

'Don't be an ass,' she muttered. 'Miles isn't the type to be bowled over by a nightdress. He's far too dedicated a doctor to see a patient as anything else.'

Yet on the other hand he was far too dedicated to see a patient only as a case; he would see them as a human being, and once the human factor came in, then emotion could creep in too.

Her thoughts became more disquieting and she was glad when lunchtime came around, and decided to close the office and use the time to buy herself a new dress for her date with Miles the following evening. Something diaphanous, she decided as she locked the door and pinned a note on it saying she would be back at two-thirty.

The shops in the vicinity were too large to offer the individual service she preferred, and because time was short she took a taxi to Knightsbridge and wandered down the small turnings and past various individual boutiques where she usually bought her clothes. In her favourite one she found what she wanted: a pale silk jersey dress, the colour of cream, whose long flowing lines were guaranteed to raise the wolf in the most sheepish of men.

Carrying the parcel with her, she returned to Bond Street. The dress was too expensive to warrant taking another taxi, so she got a bus instead. As she alighted at Fortnum's and set off along Old Bond Street, a tantalising smell of coffee reminded her that she had missed her lunch. The delicious aroma came from a small bistro and she went in, luckily securing a table by the window.

She was sipping her coffee when a tall, fair-haired man came into view with a girl on his arm. They were a good-looking couple, she thought idly, before realising with a shock that it was Roland and Gillian Denton. So much for his promise not to see the girl again!

They were too intent on each other to be aware of her watching them, and she saw they were earnestly engaged in conversation as they walked past and crossed the road, to stop outside the jewellery-filled windows of

Aspreys. Here they spoke for several more minutes before Roland leaned down and kissed Gillian, obviously saying something flattering, for it brought a happy smile to her face. Then he hailed a taxi and got in, and Gillian waved to him until the cab had disappeared before she went into Aspreys alone.

Without stopping to think, Natalie rushed to the counter, paid her bill and dashed across the road. She had to see Gillian. She was not sure what she would say to her, but she could not stood by and watch Roland make a fool of the girl any longer.

Aspreys was surprisingly full and it took Natalie a moment or two before she located Gillian Denton in the men's watch department. Her apprehension grew.

'Hello, Miss Denton,' she said casually, stopping beside her. 'What a surprise to see you here!'

Gillian Denton turned and stared at Natalie blankly for an instant, then gave a wide smile.

'Why, hello there. Did you have a nice weekend?'

'It was lovely. I thought you might have come down too.'

'I was going to come, but....' Gillian stopped, and the rose pink of her cheeks gave away what she had hoped her silence would hide.

Natalie was convinced Miles's sister had seen Roland during the weekend. She might even—horror of horrors—have spent it with him! It was not the moral aspect of this which worried her as much as the fact that Roland was such an unsavoury character.

'You were with—Rodney, weren't you?' Natalie stated matter-of-factly, and this time the colour left Gillian's face.

'You—you know him?'

'He's the brother of my closest friend. At the moment

Maggie is in hospital and I'm looking after her office.' Then she said deliberately: 'It's a marriage bureau. His name is Roland Whitney, not Rodney White.'

Astonishment kept Gillian speechless. Then other emotions flitted over her face and the colour seeped back into it.

'Was that how you met Miles? You work with your friend and—and....'

'Only temporarily while Maggie's ill.' Natalie was aware of one of the assistants watching them. 'I'd very much like to talk to you, Miss Denton. Have you time for a cup of coffee with me?'

'Is it any use my saying we have nothing to talk about?' Gillian asked resignedly, and with a brief murmur to the assistant that she would be back later, she followed Natalie across the road to the café where, fortunately, the window table was still empty.

Only when two cups of coffee had been set before them did Natalie speak, plunging in without worrying about diplomacy, knowing that what she had to say must be said bluntly.

'Your brother came to the Whitney Marriage Bureau because he was furious that we'd introduced you to someone who he considered was up to no good.'

'My brother thinks all my boy-friends are no good.'

'In Roland's case, he isn't wrong.'

'What has he done that's so terrible?' Gillian asked defiantly.

'Would you believe me if I told you?' Natalie answered grimly, and then continued before the girl could reply. 'He went to Australia because it was getting too hot for him here, and I think he probably came back for the same reason. He's too clever to do anything that's outright criminal, but one day he'll overstep the mark.'

'But what has he *done*?' Gillian demanded.

'Sold dud cars, passed dud cheques, conned rich old women—and now rich young ones.'

'You've no right to say that!'

'Haven't I? I know he met you under false pretences and told you he'd been given your name by the Whitney Marriage Bureau. I also know you've been buying him expensive presents and that he's resold one of them. Cufflinks,' Natalie added for good measure.

'Because he needed the money and didn't like to ask me for it. What's so terrible about that? Anyway, once I'd given them to him he could do what he liked with them.'

'You don't honestly believe that, do you?' Natalie said scornfully. 'A five-hundred-pound pair of cufflinks isn't something one sells immediately one gets them. Not unless he'd angled for them in the first place.'

'He didn't angle,' said Gillian. 'I gave them to him for his birthday. But he had some debts to pay and he —he wanted to start off with a clean slate.'

'A new girl-friend and a new leaf?'

'Is that so hard to believe?'

'With Roland—yes.' Natalie shook her head. 'Maggie's wiped countless slates clean for him already, but it hasn't stopped him from messing up another one straight away. He's no good, Miss Denton. Neither to you nor to any other girl.'

'What gives you the right to organise my life?' Gillian asked. 'Just because you're going out with Miles it doesn't——'

'My seeing Miles has nothing to do with it. I'm telling

you about Roland because I don't want you to be hurt.'

'That's my business. And I wish you'd mind your own!' Gillian snapped, and at once looked discomfited. 'I'm sorry, I didn't mean to be rude, but I really don't need you to give me any advice.'

'You need it,' Natalie corrected, 'but you obviously won't take it. I'm sure Miles has already spoken to you, but if you won't listen to *him*, I suppose it's too much to hope you will listen to me. But I had to try, especially when I saw you and Roland together. I should have known he wouldn't keep his promise not to see you any more.'

'When did he promise that?'

'When your brother threatened to put our bureau out of business.'

'What?' Gillian looked furious. 'How dare Miles make a threat like that!'

'He was quite within his rights,' Natalie replied, and spared an instant to marvel that she should be defending Miles's action. 'I would have done exactly the same in his position. If he reported the Whitney Bureau to the Council, my friend could be in serious trouble. Roland had no business to go through the files and seach for your telephone number, and then pretend he was an introduction from us.'

'I'm not saying Rod—Roland was right,' Gillian said stubbornly, 'but I don't see that it was so criminal. In any case, this is all in the past.'

'What about the future?' Natalie asked. 'It wouldn't be a very pleasant one for you if you're thinking of sharing it with Roland.' She leaned forward, unconsciously using the girl's first name. 'You're not, are you, Gillian?'

'I haven't thought that far ahead.' The reply was

muted, as if the girl were unwilling to speak a lie with any force.

'Well, do so,' Natalie pleaded. 'Roland's no good. Make your own enquiries about him if you don't want to believe me. He hasn't got a job, nor was it his birthday when he accepted the cufflinks as a present from you.'

'He's already told me that himself,' Gillian said. 'I know you're talking to me like this for my own good, but I'm not a child. That's something Miles has never seemed to realise. I'll be nineteen in a few weeks, and lots of girls are already married at that age.'

'Lots of girls at that age have been earning a living for several years, not living in rich idleness.' Natalie was deliberately rude, feeling that she might as well go the whole hog and tell Gillian a few more home truths. There was nothing to be lost and there might still be something to be gained. 'You've led a sheltered life, and you're extremely young for your age. If you weren't, you would have seen through Roland yourself. And if you believe that the only way to keep him is to buy him expensive presents, then you're a stupid fool!'

'What a hateful thing to say!' Gillian cried, and stared down at her coffee cup with her eyes masked. She did not look nearly so much like Miles, and Natalie's exasperation with her grew. The little fool deserved what she'd get if she tied herself up with a rotter like Roland. Then Gillian tilted her head, and as she saw the golden irises, Natalie's heart seemed to turn over in her breast and she wished she could retract everything she had just said.

'I suppose you won't believe I'm talking to you like this for your own good.'

'Well, it certainly can't be for *your* good.' Gillian was searching in her handbag for her handkerchief. 'Since you know I won't listen to Miles, I can't think why you should imagine I'll listen to you.'

'Because at least my opinion is unbiased. Look, Gillian, if you do intend to continue seeing Roland, can't you at least behave like a normal nineteen-year-old and let *him* do the chasing?'

'He's been doing the chasing,' Gillian said instantly. 'I never ring him up.'

'But you spend money on him,' Natalie said gently.

'Only because he hasn't found a job yet.'

'He isn't penniless.' Natalie put some money on the table and stood up. 'I can't prevent you seeing him, but I hope you won't go on buying his company.'

'How dare you say that?'

'Prove me wrong, then. See if he still wants you if you keep your hands in your pockets. My bet is that after a few dates where he's the one to fork out the cash, he'll go back to his old ways and his old women!'

Without waiting for Gillian to reply, Natalie stormed out and was halfway up Bond Street before her temper had cooled sufficiently for her to regret the loss of it. She didn't have red hair for nothing, she thought wryly.

She was unlocking the door of the office when she heard the telephone ringing, and she rushed across to answer it, trembling with pleasure when she heard Miles's voice.

'Where on earth have you been?' he demanded. 'This is the second time I've tried to get you.'

'I went out to lunch. I've only just got back.'

'It must have been a very successful lunch.'

She glanced at her watch and saw it was three o'clock.

She was on the verge of telling him she had been with his sister, when she stopped. If she mentioned Gillian, it would mean mentioning Roland, and she did not want to do this over the telephone.

'Are you busy?' she asked, just happy to talk to him, and not really caring what she said.

'I'm up to my eyes,' he replied, 'but I had to hear your voice. You wouldn't be free tonight, by any chance?'

'It just so happens I would.' She was so delighted she could have stood on her head, though some of her delight evaporated as she remembered she had planned to see Maggie.

'What time were you thinking of?' she asked.

'Then you do have something else to do?'

'I was going to pop in on Maggie,' she admitted.

'I'll take you.'

'I wouldn't dream of letting you,' she said with a laugh. 'That would be a busman's holiday for you. I'll go and see Maggie and then meet you back at your flat.'

'What an excellent idea.' His voice was so full of humour that she knew instantly he was grinning from ear to ear.

Her mouth curved in an answering smile. 'Maybe it's not such a good idea. Let's meet in a restaurant instead. I take it the invitation did include dinner?'

'What a girl you are for thinking of her stomach!' This time he chuckled audibly. 'Let's meet at my flat at eight-thirty and then go on to the Berkeley.'

A step in the outer office made her turn her head and Roland came into the office.

'That's a date. Be seeing you,' she said quickly, and put down the receiver.

'Chatting up the boy-friend?' Roland said easily.

'What do you want?' she asked pointedly.

'Fifty quid. I have to see a man about a very expensive dog.'

'When are you seeing a man about a job?'

'I have several in the offing, but there's no point rushing into something.' He sat down, elegant as always in a faultlessly cut suit, his expression bland. 'You look blooming, Natalie old girl. Being in love must agree with you.'

'I'm not in love.'

'Then how come you spent the weekend with Miles Denton?' He grinned as he saw her discomfiture. 'You shouldn't try to keep secrets from your Uncle Roland.'

'It isn't a secret,' she snapped, 'and I didn't spend the weekend with him. I was staying with his mother.'

'Curiouser and curiouser.' Roland was openly mocking. 'Now I know he must be serious about you. When a man like Denton takes you home to meet his mum....'

Ignoring him, Natalie reached for her cheque book and wrote out a cheque. 'If you want any more money after this,' she said, handing it to him, 'you'll have to deal with Maggie. I don't intend to keep subsidising you on her behalf.'

'I'll pay it all back when my ship comes in.'

'Not if it's the good ship Gillie!' Natalie said bitingly. 'If she sets sail with you, it will be without a cargo—her brother will see to that.'

'My, you are sharp today,' said Roland admiringly. 'But luckily your threats don't bother me. Or have you forgotten it isn't the business of the pot to call the kettle black?'

'I don't know what you mean by that,' Natalie red. 'But you gave me your word you'd stop seeing

Gillian, and because of that, Miles Denton didn't get our licence taken away. If he finds out you've broken your promise he'll——'

'He won't find out,' Roland interrupted, 'because you aren't going to tell him.'

'I most certainly will,' Natalie said angrily. 'I'll also tell him to stop his sister's allowance. If you want to go on seeing her you'll have to pay for the pleasure. And let me remind you that she's barely nineteen and doesn't inherit her money until she's twenty-five. So if you're planning a future with her, you'll have to earn your living for the next six years at least.' Natalie's voice was heavy with scorn. 'And since I don't believe you're capable of earning your living for six months, it will give Gillian ample time to realise what a no-good swine you are long before she comes into her fortune.'

'You've got everything worked out, haven't you?' Roland sneered, and leaned back in his chair.

It was an oddly composed gesture for one who ought to be looking discomfited, and with a faint stab of fear Natalie wondered what trick he had left to play. She was not left long in doubt.

'Before you start dishing out the threats, old thing,' he drawled, 'you should make sure of your own position. If you tell Big Brother I'm still seeing his sister, he won't need to go and get the Bureau's licence taken away, because I'll do it for him.'

Natalie glared at him in disbelief. 'You'll what?'

'If you tell on me, I'll tell on you.'

'What's there to tell? I haven't done anything wrong.'

'Only started going out with a client—which is exactly what you accuse *me* of doing.'

Natalie opened her mouth to deny what Roland had said, then closed it again.

'You see how easy it is to make a mistake,' he went on triumphantly. 'I came up to the office last week when you weren't here, and had a little look around.'

'How did you get in?'

'With a key.' He reached into his pocket and held it out to show her. 'What I found out was very interesting. Miles Denton is on your books as a client. At least the receipt book shows he paid the fee for going on the books, so I assume he must be looking for a wife.'

'He happened to be looking for——' Natalie stopped, knowing that to tell Roland Miles had wanted someone for Gayle would furnish him with yet another possible source of mischief.

'Miles gave me that money for something private,' she said.

'The exact amount it costs to enrol? You'll have to do better than that, old thing.'

'Stop calling me "old thing"!'

'Sorry,' he smiled, and folded his arms across his chest. 'Anyway, no matter what you say the money was for, I'm prepared to go to the Council and say it was because he wanted you to find him a wife. I don't blame you for putting yourself forward—after all, he's a good catch—but I don't think the Council would approve of your methods.'

'If you went to them with a story like that, I'd tell them you were lying.'

'They might believe you,' he replied, 'but on the other hand they might not. If you're prepared to take a gamble on it....'

Natalie stared at him. 'Would you really go and chance ruining Maggie's business?'

'That's up to you.' Roland returned her stare. 'If you don't interfere with me, I won't interfere with you.'

'But you can't be serious about Gillian Denton!'

'Does that mean you're serious about Big Brother?' His smile was foxy. 'My, my, no wonder you're so hot under the collar!' He rose and strolled over to the desk. 'Look here, Natalie, the last thing I want is to queer your pitch. If you can bring him to the boil, good luck to you. But leave me alone to go on seeing Gillie. I promise I won't marry her.'

'You just intend to use her,' Natalie accused.

'She loves me,' he said smugly, 'and I find her amusing and pretty.'

'And rich.'

'And rich,' he agreed. 'But I'm giving you the choice. Forget about my seeing Gillian and I'll forget you're seeing her brother. It's as simple as that.' He paused by the door. 'Enjoy yourself this evening, old thing.'

The door closed and Natalie stared at it for a long time before getting up and going over to the filing cabinet. She looked through the folder marked 'D' and found the receipt she had made out for Miles Denton. If only she had not accepted the enrolment money from him! But when he had asked her to find a boy-friend for Gayle, he had thrown a wad of notes on to the desk and curtly told her to make it a business transaction. Stupidly she had not made out the enrolment in Gayle's name, but to Miles himself, and here was a copy of the receipt she had given him. But why was it a photo-copy? Where was the actual one?

It required little intelligence to know it was reposing somewhere among Roland's possessions. So much for her hope of destroying it!

Closing the filing cabinet, she sat down. She was shaking with nerves and she tried to calm herself. She had to think clearly, not only because of Maggie, but for her own future with Miles. Both would be safe providing she kept her mouth shut and allowed Roland to continue seeing Gillian Denton. Damn the girl! Let her make a fool of herself.

'I can't,' Natalie said aloud, and hearing her voice in the quietness of the room, acknowledged ruefully that conscience would not let her keep quiet. She would tell Maggie the whole story. If Maggie then spoke to Roland he would surely not have the gall to admit that he would shop his own sister.

On this hopeful thought, Natalie felt better able to face the afternoon, and was glad when telephone calls and a tentative visit from an elderly woman seeking a husband kept her too occupied to think of anything other than the business in hand.

CHAPTER NINE

As Natalie walked along the hospital corridor, she saw the rawboned figure of Angus walking towards her.

'You're just the man I want to see,' she said, impulsively deciding to tell him of her problem and ask whether it would be wise to burden her friend with it. 'Do you have a few minutes to spare?'

Seeing from her expression that something was wrong, he drew her into a small office alongside the ward, and listened intently as she told him of Roland's latest threat and her desire to enlist Maggie's help in stopping him.

'You daren't worry her with all this,' Angus said emphatically. 'She's still suffering from hypertension, and if she thought her business might be knocked out from under her—by her own brother too—it could give her a relapse.'

'I didn't realise she was still so ill,' Natalie said in dismay.

'Maggie's the type who hides her symptoms until she reaches breaking point and collapses.'

'How long will it be before she's well?'

'She should be leaving hospital in ten days, but I don't think she'll be fit for at least a month.' He pressed his lips. 'She needs to convalesce somewhere.'

'She can stay with me,' Natalie said instantly.

'In a flat in London? That isn't what I mean by convalescing. I'm going to suggest she stays with my parents in Stirling.'

Natalie looked startled. 'Isn't it rather cold up there?'

'Not at this time of the year. Anyway, Maggie's a hardy Scot. And besides,' he added casually, 'I shall be taking my holiday round about the same time, so I'll be able to see she obeys doctor's orders.'

There was something in his tone that told Natalie the orders would include a loving embrace from time to time, and she hoped wholeheartedly that the romance she suspected was, in fact, blossoming.

'I know you're in a tricky position,' Angus went on, patting Natalie's hand awkwardly, 'but you've coped so well that another month won't make all that difference. Apart from which, I don't see why you should feel responsible for Gillian Denton.'

'Because I like Miles, and if I don't tell him his sister is still seeing Roland, he will be furious with me.'

'He won't be furious when you tell him the reason you kept quiet.'

It was a logical assertion, but it did not give Natalie much comfort. Miles would feel that in not telling him about Roland at once, she had acted deceitfully. He would probably even say she had put her friendship for Maggie before her feelings for him. Yet though this was true, didn't Maggie's illness make this justifiable behaviour? Surely Miles, as a surgeon, would appreciate this?

'Cheer up,' Angus urged. 'Things aren't that bad.'

'They could get worse,' she agreed dolefully. 'What happens if Gillian marries Roland?'

'I thought you said she doesn't get her money for another six years?'

'It might not stop Roland. Once she was his wife he'd bank on the fact that the Dentons wouldn't stand by and see her living in penury.'

'So why should you care? She might even be happy with him.'

'Never. He's a real swine. If Gillian married him, Miles would never forgive me for keeping quiet.'

Angus looked at Natalie with dawning wonderment. 'You're in love with Denton, aren't you? I hadn't realised that. No wonder you're so concerned about his sister!' He ran a hand through his rough red hair. 'But I still hope you won't tell Maggie. If she makes good progress I'll tell her the story myself. I'll even go and see Roland and try to knock some sense into him, if you like.'

'It isn't sense that should be knocked into him,' Natalie said grimly, 'it's decency.'

Resolutely she set off in the direction of Maggie's ward, aware of Angus watching her but still not sure whether she could abide by his wishes. It was only when she saw Maggie sitting up against the pillows, her face pinched and devoid of colour, that she knew she would do as he asked, regardless of how difficult it made her own position.

'Hello there,' she said briskly, placing a box of chocolates on the bedside table and pulling up a chair. 'You're looking heaps better.'

'Liar,' Maggie said truthfully. 'I look dreadful, though I must admit I feel much better.'

'Then that's all that counts. Once you're out of here you'll soon get your colour back. I hear Stirling is very bracing.'

Maggie looked embarrassed. 'I haven't yet agreed to Angus's suggestion. I'll only go if you don't mind staying on at the Bureau a bit longer. If you can't, for heaven's sake be honest and say so. I feel guilty enough for ruining your holiday.'

'I told you I wasn't going to have one. Moving flats cost me so much money that working at the Bureau is just what I need. As long as you come back before my school starts again, I'm fine.'

'I'll be back long before then,' Maggie promised. 'Angus wants me to stay with his parents for a month, but I shall only make it two weeks.'

Natalie was silent, certain that once Maggie was in Scotland, Angus would make sure she remained there until she was completely well. Without realising it she sighed, and her friend looked at her anxiously.

'Things are all right at the Bureau, aren't they, Nat? You're not hiding anything from me?'

'They couldn't be better,' Natalie smiled, and brought out a bundle of letters from appreciative clients.

Maggie read them and then put them in her bedside drawer. 'I'll show them to Angus,' she murmured softly. 'He's always saying marriage bureaus are a waste of time.'

'Let him enrol and find out for himself. We've got loads of lady clients who'd give their eye-teeth to meet an eligible doctor—even if he *is* a rawboned Scot!'

'He isn't rawboned,' Maggie said indignantly, then knowing she had fallen into Natalie's trap, she gave a tremulous laugh. 'You're a beast, Nat!'

'But a clever one. Angus has his eye on you, so put on the poor little invalid act, and he'll be eating out of your hand.'

Maggie smiled and, refusing to rise to any further baiting, changed the conversation, unfortunately bringing it round to Roland.

'He hasn't been in to see me this week. I do hope he's not in any trouble.'

'He's in the pink of condition,' Natalie said without expression. 'I gave him another fifty pounds to tide him over and he hopes to find a job pretty soon. If he doesn't,' she went on, determined that ill or not, Maggie shouldn't live in a total fool's paradise, 'you'd be crazy if you gave him another penny.'

'I know. Being ill has made me face the truth about him.'

'Good. Now all you need do is to get well and come back to the office. Your new clients need you.'

'Not as much as I need them,' Maggie sighed. 'My lease comes up for renewal soon, and I must make up my mind whether or not I should continue with the Bureau.'

Natalie's heart thumped loudly. If Maggie was not going to carry on, it would not matter if the licence was taken away. That meant it would be possible to tell Miles about his sister and Roland.

'However, if you were being truthful about all the new clients we have,' Maggie broke into Natalie's thoughts, 'then I'll write to the landlords and say I want to renew my tenancy. That's why it's important for me to know you aren't just trying to reassure me.'

'I'll bring you all the cards of the new clients,' Natalie replied, 'then you can see for yourself.'

The relief on Maggie's face was great, and afraid that her own disappointment might show, Natalie stood up.

'Must you leave so soon?' Maggie pleaded.

'I have a date.'

Natalie did not say with whom, but gave her friend a hug and promised to come and see her again within a few days.

It was exactly half past eight when she rang the door of Miles's house. She noticed again how resplendent it was, as was he, as the door swung back and he stood before her in a superbly cut navy suit. The darkness emphasised his pallor and narrow patrician features. He was not a man to take deceit lightly, she thought, noticing the firm line of his mouth and jaw, and found herself unable to meet his eyes as she stepped into the house.

'A punctual woman,' he commented, taking hold of her hand. 'Don't you have any vices—apart from your dreadful temper?'

She made herself smile. 'I've occasionally been known to throw things, but I never hit the object of my dislike!'

He chuckled and led her towards the small lift. 'I thought we would have a drink here and then go out to dinner—unless you'd rather go out right away?'

Unwilling to face the intimacy of being alone with him, she said she would prefer to go out, and knew that her swift answer had surprised and disappointed him.

'I've put some champagne on ice,' he said, 'but if you're hungry....'

'I am rather,' she lied, and waited as he closed the lift door again and led her back across the hall and out of the house.

'I didn't book at the Berkeley after all,' he said. 'As we were meeting here, I thought we'd go to a small Italian restaurant close by. A colleague reminded me of it this afternoon and I thought you might find it more amusing than an hotel.'

'I like Italian food,' Natalie smiled.

'If you'd also like a five-minute walk, we needn't take the car.'

She nodded, hoping the fresh air would blow away

her feelings of guilt and enable her to act more naturally with him. If it didn't, the evening ahead was going to be a difficult one, for he had noticed her constraint and it was affecting his own attitude. Side by side they walked down Harley Street and she was conscious of how tall he was, easily topping her own five feet six inches and making her feel unusually petite.

'Do you ever get backache?' she asked.

'Backache?' He looked surprised by the question.

'Because of having to bend over the operating table.'

'We have it at working height,' he said with some amusement. 'Unlike the average housewife, I don't have to put up with wrong kitchen equipment!'

She laughed. 'It was a silly question for me to ask.'

'None of your questions are silly, Natalie. You have a good brain.' He put his hand under her elbow to guide her across the road and then kept it there. 'What made you decide to become a nursery school teacher, instead of a model or something equally glamorous?'

'I would hate to be a model or anything else that you call glamorous. I've always liked children. I've even written stories for them,' she confessed, glad to be able to talk about a subject which wasn't dangerous. 'As a matter of fact I've written a book of children's stories and have even found a publisher who's keen to do them as soon as he can find a suitable illustrator.'

'That's marvellous.' Miles sounded genuinely delighted. 'You must let me read them. Do you have a copy of your manuscript?'

'Yes, but I'm afraid you would find them rather childish.'

'I know you didn't write them for fogey old surgeons,' he smiled, 'but I would like to read them nonetheless. It will make me feel I know you better.'

His fingers gently squeezed her elbow and her guilt increased. Damn Roland! He was going to sour what could have been an ideal friendship that might—if she were lucky—have led to much more.

'Here we are,' said Miles, stopping outside a narrow-fronted Georgian house, in a cul-de-sac bordering on Regent's Park.

'What an unusual place for a restaurant!' she exclaimed.

'It's an unusual restaurant. Those who know it keep quiet about it in case it gets so popular that its standards deteriorate.'

They went up the shallow steps into a narrow hall, and thence into a room that ran the entire depth of the house. There were some dozen tables, all occupied except for the one to which they were shown.

Several pairs of interested eyes watched them and three people nodded at Miles.

'I always meet people I know here,' he explained briefly. 'The man we passed just now is a colleague of mine at the hospital.'

'That reminds me,' said Natalie, 'how is Sir Elton?'

'In the best of spirits. In fact he asked me to give you his best wishes.'

'He knows you're still seeing me?'

'Of course.'

'Of course,' she echoed, and tried not to feel despondent. 'That's the whole object of the exercise.'

'That was the original object,' Miles corrected, and might have said more if the waiter had not chosen that moment to approach their table with the menus.

Natalie took one and brandished it in front of her like a shield, unwilling to let Miles see her face. 'I'll just have a steak and salad,' she said. 'And melon to begin with, please.'

'That sounds like a dieter's dinner,' Miles smiled and, leaning forward, tipped down her menu in order to stare at her more closely. 'Are you feeling well tonight, Natalie? Or has the visit to the hospital upset you? Is your friend worse?'

'Oh no, she's fine. And I'm not upset in the least.' Hurriedly she continued to speak. 'Maggie is going up to Stirling to convalesce next week. She's stopping with Angus's parents. Angus is the Registrar at the hospital and has known Maggie since they were children, though they lost touch with each other for years—until her operation, in fact.'

'A fortuitous operation,' Miles smiled.

'I'm hoping so.'

'Does that mean you'll have to look after the Bureau until she returns?'

'Yes. I'll probably be there until I have to start school again.'

'I would love to see you with your toddlers,' he said softly, continuing to look into her face.

His words conjured up for her a picture of what Miles's children might be like, were he to have any, and quickly she focused on the menu again. 'I think I'll change my mind about steak—it does sound dull, I suppose—and have a veal escalope instead.'

'They do an excellent Steak Wellington here,' Miles said, 'but the portions are for two. If you would be willing to share it with me——?'

'I've never heard of a Steak Wellington,' she confessed.

'It's a small whole fillet covered with mustard and pâté and then wrapped in pastry.'

'It sounds delicious,' she smiled. 'You've talked me into it.'

'Then let me talk you into something more exciting

than melon. They do delicious seafood pancakes.'

Again she nodded, hoping the good food would help her to relax and enable her to push aside all thoughts of Roland and what he might be doing, and with whom.

Miles ordered a half bottle of Mersault followed by a bottle of Burgundy, which did more than the food to help her forget Roland, and by the time she was sipping her coffee, she was quite relaxed. It was only when he started to talk about his sister that her guilt flooded back.

'I never thought I would be grateful for Gillian's erratic choice of boy-friends,' Miles said. 'But if she hadn't gone to the Whitney Bureau, it might have taken me much longer to find you.'

'You might never have found me,' she smiled.

'I refuse to believe that. It was in the stars that we would meet.'

'I'm sure you don't believe in the stars!'

'I don't,' he grinned, 'but most women do. Even my Registrar, who is a highly efficient, logical lady, admits that she reads her horoscope every day. She says she only does it for fun, but I'm sure she half believes it.'

'Do you only believe in things that can be proved?'

'It depends what you mean by proof. But I refuse to believe that stars, millions and millions of light years away from us, can have any effect upon our behaviour. I suppose you think that's very prosaic of me?'

'Yes, I do. But it's what I expected. You're a logical man, Miles. It's part of your training. I shouldn't think you believe in intuition either.'

'You're wrong there. I do believe in it, only I call it lightning fast deduction. That's what intuition is—the ability of the brain to unconsciously assimilate all facts, and hundreds of little nuances that lead it to come to a conclusion with the rapidity of a computer.'

'Oh dear!' She pulled a face. 'So Gemini intuition goes by the board too. What else don't you believe?'

'Romantic love,' he said promptly. 'It's a hoax dreamed up by the advertising media. Men and women marry because they want companionship or a family or someone to take care of them. The belief that only one particular man or woman can appease your need is utter rot.'

Natalie forced herself to remain silent, though she longed to annihilate his argument. A hoax of the advertising media, indeed! The man must be mad. Were Shakespeare's sonnets a hoax? Or the Psalms of David? And what about the thousands—the millions of people who shared their lives with the partners of their choice and were desolate when they died? Miles could not mean what he said. Feminine intuition—which he deplored so forcibly—told her he was only speaking like this in an effort to fight against the deep attraction he felt for her. Putting it on a mundane level was his way of trying to retain his detachment.

'Well,' he questioned, 'aren't you going to make any comment?'

'Only that you sound like a man who is struggling with himself,' she said without any expression in her voice or on her face.

'How damn right you are!' His own look was rueful. 'Until a few days ago I believed everything I just said. Love was for others—not me. I was one of the lucky ones who lived on an entirely different plane. I could go through my life taking only what I wanted to take.'

'And now?'

'Now I find I've been taken. You know what I'm saying to you, don't you, Natalie?'

To have denied it would have made her look more naïve than he would have believed possible. Yet if she admitted she understood him, he would expect her to give voice to her own feelings about him, and she found it impossible to do this while she was still unable to tell him that Roland was at this very moment trying to seduce his sister. Love meant truth and frankness, not lies and secrecy.

'Is the question I asked you so difficult to answer?' Miles murmured.

'I'm not sure what to say,' she blurted out.

'Then say nothing.'

His voice was matter-of-fact, but it did not hide the bleakness in his eyes, and she knew he was hurt that, having confessed his own feelings, she should find it so difficult to confess hers; or perhaps he thought she did not love him.

'Miles, I——'

'Don't say anything,' he cut in swiftly. 'I've rushed you and I'm sorry. I tend to forget that other people sometimes take longer to make up their minds about things.'

'Have you never regretted a quick decision?'

'No.' It was a clipped sound. 'But I do know when to retract.'

'Don't retract this time,' she said quickly. 'I'm just asking you to—to temporarily withdraw.'

'By all means.' He was polite and distant, and with a shuttered look on his face he signalled the waiter to bring their bill.

Slowly they walked back along the dark streets. Lamplight threw mellow silver pools on the pavement and the air was warm but dusty.

'I envy your mother living in the country,' she said softly. 'Don't you ever feel you would like to live out of town?'

'Quite often. But it isn't convenient for a bachelor to do that. In Harley Street I have everything at my fingertips—my consulting room, my home, a housekeeper, a secretary.'

He hesitated, as if wishing to say something more, then he quickened his step, so that by the time Natalie reached his house she was almost breathless.

'Will you come up for a drink?' Miles asked perfunctorily, 'or do you want me to take you home straight away?'

Common sense told her to say she would go home, but she was afraid that if she left him while he was in this mood, she might never hear from him again. Mutely she looked at the door, and interpreting the gesture correctly, he unlocked it and led her inside. Silently they went up to the top floor in the lift and along the thickly carpeted passage to the sitting room.

As always its opulent modernity dismayed her, though it was softened by the rose-shaped lamps.

'I don't think this room is in character with you,' she said, sinking down on to the settee.

'I don't like it either, but I'm never here long enough to let it worry me.' He went to the sideboard. 'Shall I open the champagne, or would you prefer a brandy?'

'Actually I don't want anything.'

'Neither do I,' he said, and swinging round abruptly, came over to sit beside her. 'I wanted you to come up here with me,' he went on, 'but I had to give you the opportunity to refuse.'

'Why?'

'Because I wasn't sure if you wanted me as much as I want you.'

She was quick to notice he did not use the word love, but in view of her earlier lack of forthcomingness, she could not blame him. She felt the slow beating of his heart. Its steadiness was reassuring and gave her unexpected courage. Regardless of what anyone else said, she had to tell him about Roland.

'Miles, I want to talk to you.'

'Kiss me first,' he said throatily. 'You've done nothing the whole evening except talk.'

Abruptly he covered her mouth with his own, at the same time lying back upon the settee and pulling her on top of him. Her hair swung forward, the silken strands enveloping him in a fragrant cloud of dark red. She felt the warmth of his hands through the thin crêpe of her dress and was very conscious of the soft fullness of her breasts resting upon his chest. She moved slightly, but his grip tightened and he pulled her closer still.

'You're very enticing,' he whispered against her lips.

'And you're very strong.'

'With you, I feel like Samson.'

'Before or after he had his locks shorn?'

She felt his breath as he chuckled. 'Definitely after! You've made me weak, but I don't regret it.'

'How weak?'

'Strong enough for this,' he said huskily, lowering her zip.

The bodice of her dress fell away from her shoulders and he was instantly aware that she wore no bra. His breath came out on a half sigh of longing, then he placed his lips between the shadowed hollow and moved them along a creamy curve to the pink-centred heart. It stiffened at his touch and, aware of it, his need of her became too apparent for her to ignore.

'Miles, I——'

The telephone bell cut across her words and Miles sat up and gently lifted her away from him before reaching out for the receiver.

'Denton speaking,' he said softly, and then listened.

Watching him, Natalie saw the perceptible change in his body: a stiffening of the muscles and a tightening of the jaw line as his adrenalin began to flow and the would-be lover gave way to the surgeon.

'I'll be with you in ten minutes,' he said into the telephone. 'Prepare the theatre. You did right to call me.' He replaced the receiver and rose at the same time. 'I have an emergency operation at the hospital.'

'I'll see myself home,' Natalie said quickly, and knew from the blank look he gave her that he had not even considered doing so himself. She was no longer in his mind, but she was not hurt by the knowledge. It would always be like this. No matter how intimate the occasion between them, there would always be one part of his brain poised, ready for the moment of danger to be signalled. This, after all, was what he had been trained for, and what was the very fabric of his life.

'I'm sorry, Natalie.' He was moving to the door as he spoke.

'Don't apologise for being a surgeon,' she replied, and preceded him into the lift. 'Would you like me to come to the hospital with you and wait?' she asked as they reached the street.

'Good heavens, no! I might be a couple of hours. But you can come with me and get a taxi from the hospital. I don't want to leave you standing here.'

'I'll be fine,' she said, realising he did not really want

her to go with him. He needed to marshall his thoughts for the operation ahead. 'Do go, Miles.' She glanced up the road. 'I can see a taxi coming, it will be here in a moment.'

With a nod Miles slipped in front of the wheel. She watched the tail lights of his car disappear around the corner, then ignoring the taxi slowly chugging towards her, she began to walk in the direction of Oxford Street.

If only the telephone had rung a few moments later and given her the chance to talk to Miles about Roland! What a fool she had been to hesitate and not tell him the truth at dinner. If Miles loved her—and she was sure now that he did—he would definitely not do anything to harm Maggie. Nor would he believe that she herself had anything whatever to do with Roland's siege of Gillian. This seemed so clear to her now that she was astonished it had not been clear to her before. But perhaps it had needed Miles's show of passionate tenderness to give her the confidence to know she could be truthful without his doubting her.

She slowed her steps, savouring the few moments they had had together and revelling in the memory of his touch and the feel of his body. She thought of getting to know him better and knew that their courtship was going to be a fast and heady one. 'I make up my mind quickly,' he had said, and she knew it to be true, for they had barely known one another a couple of weeks.

Another taxi chugged past and this time she signalled it to stop and climbed in. Where would her home be in three months' time? The question brought a smile to her lips and she stared unseeingly through the window, her mind too busy with the future to give much thought to the present.

CHAPTER TEN

INSTEAD of the two hours Miles had anticipated, the operation took him four, and for several dark moments it had looked as if he might lose the patient completely. Even now he was not sure the man would pull through the next critical seventy-two hours. But he had done his best, and now it was in the hands—if hands they could be called—of the electronic machines that would monitor every breath and heartbeat, every fluctuation in the man's system.

Wearily Miles walked across the hospital courtyard to his car. The night air had freshened and a slight breeze ruffled his hair, but the smell of ether still clung to him and stood for a moment by the bonnet before climbing in and starting for home.

He was bone-tired from concentration, yet he knew that when he went to bed he would be unable to sleep. He would lie wakeful, going over every step of the operation he had just done. He frowned. Rarely did he allow himself to reach the state he was in tonight, and normally he would have seen it as a sign that he needed a holiday. Yet he had returned from one barely two months ago and he knew his restlessness and tension was due to the emotional state in which his unexpected feelings for Natalie had put him.

The very thought of her name conjured up each rounded curve of her, each flowing line so clearly etched in his mind that his fingers curled round the wheel almost as if they were touching her body. And now he longed to touch it! If the telephone had not disturbed them tonight, heaven alone knew what would have happened. He gave a slight smile. It didn't require heaven to tell him such a thing, since he knew only too well for himself. God, he wanted her! But more than that, he needed her. It was a surprising admission—as surprising as when he had first acknowledged to himself that this young woman had got under his skin. If he were not a cautious man he would have asked her to marry him tonight, and it was her own unexpected coolness during dinner which had stopped him.

He loved her—that much he knew—but he regarded marriage as a binding contract not to be lightly entered, and though his heart told him he loved Natalie the way he had loved no other woman, his brain counselled caution. The same caution that had kept his knife poised above his patient tonight. The hesitation had probably saved a life, and he saw this as an omen for his own behaviour.

Don't rush things, he warned himself. See as much of Natalie as she'll allow; if things work out well, you can still be married by the end of the year. The idea of waiting four months made him groan, and hearing the sound in the confines of his car, he smiled. As the walls of Jericho had tumbled down at the sound of the trumpets of the Israelites, so had his defences crumbled at the sound of Natalie's voice. All his preconceived ideas of remaining a carefree bachelor had been dissolved by one look from her glorious eyes, one touch of her soft mouth. He savoured the pleasure that lay ahead of them both when ultimately they shared their life together.

Was he conceited to think she loved him? After all,

he was a good catch; Gayle had made that more than plain, and so had most of the other women with whom he had come into contact. Yet Natalie had treated him with scant respect—had done the opposite, in fact—which had probably appealed to him more. Her humour and sharp intelligence had kept him on the *qui vive*, and the days when he had not seen her had been long, dreary ones. He was too analytical not to have known where he was heading, but he had made no attempt to draw back—almost as if he had known that he couldn't. The bachelor status which he had cherished for so long had now become meaningless, and he could not wait to give it up. How quickly the mighty had fallen!

He slowed the car as a taxi swung sharply out of a side turning, and resisted the urge to chase after it and give the man a piece of his mind—another sign of his state of tension.

Lifting his foot from the accelerator he slowed his speed as he realised he was exceeding the limit. Maybe he was at fault and not the taxi. Chastened to realise he had been going too fast, he began to crawl, then turned left to cut through one of the squares to Oxford Street. On his right he saw the lighted entrance of a fashionable discotheque.

Several people were coming out of it, among them a slender girl with the same long, light brown hair as his sister. He glanced at the girl a second time and, as he did so, she stepped under the light of a street lamp and looked up at her companion. With an exclamation he saw it was indeed Gillian. But it was the man beside her who gave him the biggest shock, for he recognised the foxy features of Roland Whitney.

Fury almost made Miles stop the car, but somehow he

kept going, his foot on the accelerator, and drove past the couple, only slowing down as he rounded the square and turned into South Audley Street.

So much for Natalie's promise that Roland would leave Gillian alone! Her strange behaviour of tonight, which had perplexed him for a great part of the evening, suddenly became explicable. It was guilt that had made her act so awkwardly with him, and given her that oddly distraught air which he had stupidly assumed to be nervousness.

Not for one moment did it enter his head that Natalie had not known what was going on. Roland had met Gillian through the Marriage Bureau and Natalie now worked there. Equally important, she was a great friend of Roland's sister. He would not put it past them to have started the Bureau as a means of getting all three of them eligible marriage partners. It was certainly one way of meeting as many people as possible, and checking on their credentials before making any commitment.

His anger increased, directed as much at himself for his gullibility as at Natalie for causing it. Ahead of him traffic lights glowed red, and he swung his car sharply in the opposite direction and headed away from Harley Street and home towards Kensington and Natalie. It was late and she would be asleep, but he did not care. He could not rest until he saw her, and it was better to do that than lie wakeful through what was left of the night. Darn it all, if she had known Roland was still seeing Gillian, why hadn't she told him the truth?

Natalie was awakened out of a deep sleep by the insistent pealing of a bell that buzzed deep into her consciousness, causing her to thrash and turn restlessly before it finally brought her abruptly into a sitting position. For a few seconds she listened in the darkness, then sleepily she slipped on a dressing gown and slippers and padded into the hall. She peeped through the spy hole and saw with astonishment that it was Miles. Happily she shot back the bolt and opened the door.

Instantly he stepped into the hall and closed the door behind him. His face was grey with fatigue and the skin seemed so tightly stretched across the cheekbones that it gave him the look of a dead man. Only his eyes showed any sign of life, glowing with a hidden fire that made them almost blinding in their brilliance.

'What's wrong?' she gasped, and put out her hands to him. 'Did something happen to your patient? Oh, Miles....'

'I'm not here because of my patient,' he cut in. 'I'm here because of Gillian and that swine who's still seeing her.'

Natalie's hands dropped to her sides and her eyes went luminous. 'So you know?'

If there had been any lingering doubts in Miles's mind, they died that instant, and a stab of unbearable pain shot through him.

'Yes, I know. And I wish to God you'd had the guts to tell me.'

'I was afraid.'

'That I would try to stop it?'

'Of course not!' she cried. 'How could you think such a thing?'

'Then why didn't you tell me? Or did you think I'd changed my mind about him and didn't care any more?'

'I couldn't tell you. Maggie's my friend and——'

'And she's more important to you than I am,' he finished furiously.

'That's not true! Please, Miles, you're misunderstanding me.'

'I misunderstood you a long time ago. I should have known what game you were playing when you tried to stop me from taking your licence away. That was all you cared about, wasn't it? Keeping your rotten little business going regardless of what happened to Gillian!'

'Don't say things like that,' Natalie begged. 'Of course I care what happens to your sister. Why do you think I ran after her this afternoon?' She paused and gave her head a half shake. 'I mean yesterday.'

Still disorientated by the suddenness with which she had been awakened, and the tirade which Miles had unleashed upon her, she began to feel its effects and the hallway revolved around her.

'When did you see Gillian?' Miles demanded.

'After lunch—yesterday it was.' Natalie ran a shaking hand across her forehead. 'I saw her with Roland, and when they parted, I followed her. I begged her not to go on seeing him, but she wouldn't listen to me.'

'Why didn't you tell me?'

'I wanted to, but. . . .'

'But you decided against it,' Miles sneered. 'Don't bother lying to me any more. That whole marriage bureau of yours is a con. It wouldn't surprise me if you and your girl friend aren't in league with Whitney. I bet you even supply him with women to fleece, the way you supplied him with my idiot sister!'

'She's an idiot all right!' Natalie's temper had risen during this unjustified attack upon her character, and nothing could stop it from exploding. 'Is that why you woke me in the middle of the night? Because you think

Maggie and I have to go round looking for stupid girls to fall for Roland? Well, just for the record, let me tell you there are so many stupid women around that we don't need to find them for him! And I'm as stupid as the rest of them for allowing myself to be conned by *you*!'

'You're quick to try and turn the tables, aren't you?' he said furiously. 'But trying to make me feel guilty won't work. If you meant what you said, you would have told me the whole story when we had dinner this evening. But you kept quiet because you *want* Roland to stay in Gillian's life. Everything you've said to the contrary has been a lie. Maybe you're one of Roland's women too!'

'How dare you say that!' Natalie cried.

'Is it too near the truth, then?' Miles taunted.

'If you think that, then we've nothing to say to each other.'

'Don't bother playing the innocent with me! It won't wash any more. You're a clever young woman, Natalie, but not clever enough.'

'Clever?' she raged. 'I must have been the biggest fool on earth to have wanted to help you!'

'Maybe you wanted to help yourself.'

'To what?'

'To me,' he said succinctly. 'You would have to look a long way to do any better.'

'Why, you conceited....' Words failed her and she drew a shuddering breath. 'If you honestly believe what you've just said,' she continued in a trembling voice, 'then the sooner you get out of my life the better!'

'It can't be soon enough for me.' His voice was shaking too: it was a throaty sound that almost made it inaudible. 'One day I suppose I'll thank my sister for making me wake up in time. If I hadn't, I might have made the biggest mistake of my life.'

'I'm sure you'll still manage to do that,' she said tonelessly, thinking of Gayle, who would be all too willing to pick up the pieces.

As if he guessed what was going through her mind, Miles gave a bitter smile. 'I would rather have Gayle's naïvety than your cunning. She might bore me, but at least she wouldn't cheat on me.'

Natalie clenched her hands. Her temper had abated and she was overwhelmed by desolation at the thought of Miles walking out of her life in this way.

'I wanted to tell you about Roland, but I was scared. He threatened——'

'Spare me the fairy story,' Miles interrupted. 'You couldn't say anything to make me believe you.'

'Not even the truth?'

Her only answer was the quiet closing of the front door, and she stumbled back into her bedroom and collapsed in a shivering heap on the bed. Miles could not mean what he had said. He had come to her after an arduous operation, when he was at the end of his tether, both physically and emotionally. She did not know how he had discovered that Gillian was still seeing Roland, but obviously he had only just learned of it and the shock had come at a time when he was too exhausted to think clearly.

With shaking hands she pushed aside the bedclothes and climbed into bed, hoping the warmth of the covers would stop her from trembling, and knowing that the chattering of her teeth came not from cold, but from a chillness of the soul.

Miles's behaviour had nullified everything he had said earlier this evening. All his so-called love for her, his talk of the future, had been so many empty promises. When his feelings for her had been put to the test they had dissolved like snow in sunshine.

Sooner or later he would learn the truth, of course. All he needed was to talk to his sister, and once he had, he would see how unjustified his harsh accusations had been. But when that time came Natalie knew that no matter how much he pleaded with her to forgive him, she would never be able to do so.

Miles was a man who doubted a woman's integrity; whose basic distrust of the female sex was so deeply ingrained that, at the slightest test, the love he professed to feel crumbled to nothing. Certainly he had said things to her that no man had ever said before. She pulled the sheets up against her chin and lay back against the pillows. She would have given anything if she could have turned back the clock so that the last hour would cease to exist and she could go on living in a fool's paradise. But that was impossible.

For the remainder of the night Natalie lay awake, and as daylight filtered across the room, she got up and made herself some coffee, then took a hot bath in the hope that it would wash away her misery.

She was at her desk well before nine. Briskly she went through the early morning post, glad there were some half dozen letters that needed to be answered. This would occupy her for the best part of the day and stop her from wallowing in her own misery. She dared not lose her control. Once she did, she would howl like a baby.

The telephone rang and she almost jumped out of her chair. Her hand was shaking so much she could hardly lift the receiver, and only when she heard an unfamiliar voice at the other end did her nerves steady enough for her to speak. How stupid of her to suppose Miles would ring to apologise. Anyway, she could not forgive him. At least that was what she told herself, though she knew in her heart of hearts that should he ring to express any regret whatsoever, she would be more than happy to meet him halfway.

With painful silence the day dragged on, and when at last it was five-thirty, she rushed straight back to her flat, telling herself she was not doing so because she hoped Miles would call her there. Yet she knew this was exactly her reason.

Tuesday set the pattern for the rest of the week. It was not until Friday that it changed, when instead of returning home she went to see Maggie, who was leaving hospital the next morning and travelling to Stirling with Angus.

'He'll be staying for two weeks only,' Maggie explained, 'and when he comes back, so will I. So don't take any notice if he tells you I'll be there for a month. I feel heaps better already, and two weeks will be quite long enough.'

Looking at her friend's animated face, Natalie could almost believe this to be true, though Maggie's extreme slenderness still left her with some element of doubt.

'Don't commit yourself to a date of return,' she said. 'As I've already told you, I'm quite happy to stay in the Bureau until school starts again.'

Only when she was back in her own flat did Natalie admit to some regret at what she had said, knowing she would not be able to put Miles out of her mind until she left the Bureau for good. As it was, going in each day made her think of him continually. The only good thing was that Roland had kept out of her way, and though Maggie had not mentioned him, she learned from Angus that he had not even been to the hospital for ten days. With richer fish to fry, Roland could spare no time for anyone else.

The weekend went by and Natalie forced herself to go out both Saturday and Sunday. When she was in, the telephone remained balefully silent, and she found herself glaring at it as though it were alive and deliberately trying to aggravate her. She slept badly and the few hours' rest that she did manage to get were punctuated by unpleasant dreams. She might be able to keep Miles at bay during her waking hours, but at night he returned to haunt her.

She accepted invitations to two parties and on both occasions was escorted home by the most eligible young man there, which was good for her morale but not for much else, since she could not face the prospect of going out with another man so soon after Miles. It was quite crazy, for she had only known him a few weeks, yet it was impossible to get him out of her mind.

Another weekend went by and again it was Monday. There was a short note from Maggie, who seemed to be having a wonderful time and made no mention of when she was returning. There was no word from Roland either, and Natalie was curious to know what was going on and whether he was still seeing Gillian, or if Miles had successfully intervened in his sister's life.

I don't care what the Dentons do, she told herself. Only for Mrs Denton did she feel a pang of sympathy; she could imagine how dismayed that lady would be if her daughter married a man like Roland. On the other hand, if Miles married Gayle, she would at least have some compensation, Natalie thought bleakly.

Two weeks to the day that Maggie had left London,

she walked into the office. Natalie stared at her with delight.

'I told you when I'd be back,' said Maggie. 'You have no reason to look so astonished.'

'I thought Angus would persuade you to stay on.'

'The doctor in him wanted to,' Maggie said humorously, 'but the man in him couldn't bear us to be parted.' She held out her left hand, which sported a pearl and ruby antique ring on the third finger. Natalie jumped up and hugged her, delighted that at least one of them had got her man.

'I'm going to close down the Bureau,' Maggie confided some hours later, when they were comfortably sitting in a coffee bar, with time to spare before Angus was free. 'Even with our new clients we're only just keeping our heads above water, and the whole thing isn't worth the worry any more.' Her plain face became illuminated with happiness at the prospect of her future with Angus. 'I suppose you think it's old-fashioned of me to be contented just with the thought of being a wife?'

'Don't use the word "just",' Natalie said stolidly. 'For most women, being a wife and mother is a full-time occupation.'

'Would it be for you?'

'It might. But at the moment there's no man in the offing.'

'What about Miles Denton?'

The question took Natalie by surprise and she went scarlet. She had imagined her friend to be too full of her own happiness at the moment to start thinking of anyone else. But doubtless Maggie's perceptive eye had noticed her thinness and the violet shadows which fatigue had placed on her lids.

'I'm not being nosy.' Maggie did not look one whit abashed by Natalie's heightened colour. 'Angus told me about him, and he also told me what trouble you were having with Roland. You shouldn't have kept it to yourself.'

'I didn't,' Natalie retorted. 'I told that big-mouth fiancé of yours.'

Maggie gave a half smile. 'And quite rightly he told me—which is what you should have done. I appreciate why you didn't, but....' She pulled her chair closer to her friend and put her hand on Natalie's arm. 'But now I want to know the truth. You look like death warmed up, which leads me to suppose that things aren't going too well between you and Miles Denton.'

'They aren't going at all,' Natalie said with an attempt at lightness. 'We've stopped seeing each other.'

'Why?'

'For the same reason why I don't see lots of my boyfriends. One likes them for a time and then one stops liking them.'

'You don't like Miles Denton any more?'

'I loathe him!'

'Is that why you look so dreadful?' said Maggie pleasantly.

'I don't look dreadful.' Natalie took out her compact and peered at herself in its small mirror. 'I'm thinner,' she admitted, 'but I think it suits me. It makes me look ethereal.'

'Ethereal today can be ghostly tomorrow,' Maggie responded with Scottish practicality. 'Am I wrong in assuming you bowed to Roland's threats and didn't call his bluff?'

Natalie put down her compact and stared at her

friend in dismay. 'Angus really has been talking, hasn't he?'

'Since I'm giving up the Bureau he saw no point in not telling me.' Maggie sighed. 'It wasn't easy for him to tell me my brother is a first-class rotter. But at least knowing I have Angus makes it easier for me to bear.'

'I'm delighted about that,' Natalie said sincerely.

'When did you see Roland last?' Maggie asked.

'Before you went to Scotland. I don't know if he's still seeing Gillian Denton, but it makes no difference to me. Not after the things Miles said.'

'Tell me everything that happened,' Maggie instructed.

After a moment's hesitation, compounded of embarrassment and a desire not to relive the agony of Miles's accusations, Natalie did so. To her surprise she found it good to be able to tell someone, and hearing the story aloud helped her to put it into perspective. But it did not rid her of the bitterness. Enough still remained for it to change her voice as she reached the end of the story.

'It's knowing that he thought I was pretending to like him—that I saw him as a good catch—that hurt me more than his believing I was in cahoots with Roland.'

'You can't blame the man for thinking he's a good catch,' Maggie said prosaically, 'when he so obviously is! Do you think he's taken up with Gayle Hunter again?'

'He deserves her,' Natalie snorted. 'She's a selfish bit of goods.'

'She and Roland would make an ideal couple,' Maggie grinned.

Natalie could not help laughing at the idea. 'I can't see Gayle being taken in by him. Behind those baby blue eyes of hers there's a mind like a steel trap.'

'Ready to grip on to Miles Denton?'

'I expect so.' Natalie jumped up, as if the words had caused her pain. 'Shall we go? You mustn't keep Angus waiting.'

A few moments later they were walking down Bond Street.

'I must pay you for the time you've been running the Bureau,' said Maggie.

'I don't want to be paid,' Natalie retorted. 'I helped out as a friend—nothing more.'

'I insist on giving you something,' Maggie said. 'It isn't what you deserve—I can't afford that—but at least it will help you with some expenses. And I also owe you for the money you gave to Roland. When I think of that brother of mine I could strangle him!'

'Here's your chance,' Natalie said in a tight voice, and jerked her head in the direction of the fair-haired man sauntered up the street towards them.

'Hello, Maggie,' he said, greeting her as if he had only seen her yesterday. 'I was just coming up to the office to see if you were back.'

'How kind of you to care,' his sister said dryly.

'Don't be like that, old thing. I knew you were in good hands with Angus. Which reminds me, how is he?'

'Soon to be your brother-in-law.'

'That's the best news I've heard in years!'

Roland looked genuinely pleased, and watching him, Natalie wondered at the dichotomy in his character that could make him threaten his sister harm one moment and be delighted at her happiness the next. But then Maggie seemed able to dissemble too, for she was letting Roland hug her affectionately before suddently pushing him away from her and asking:

'What's all this about you threatening to get my Bureau licence taken away?'

For a brief instant a look of comic surprise flashed across Roland's features, but he was not a con man for nothing, and he gave his sister a disarming smile.

'Natalie was silly enough to take me seriously. But I would never have done it, Sis, you know that.'

'Oh, sure,' said his sister. 'But it doesn't matter any longer, because I'm closing the business down.'

'Then all's well that ends well,' he smiled.

'How is it ending with you and Gillian Denton?' Maggie asked.

'It isn't yet.' He stared defiantly at Natalie. 'Her brother knows I'm seeing her, but he isn't interfering. So you were wrong about that, weren't you?'

'I was wrong about a lot of things,' said Natalie. 'But never wrong in thinking you were lower than a snake's belly.'

Without giving him a chance to reply she walked away, and Maggie caught up with her a moment later.

'I'm sorry we bumped into him, Nat,' she apologised. 'I don't blame you for feeling the way you do. But he's still my brother and I can't cut him out of my life.'

'I don't expect you to do that.'

Natalie touched her friend's arm to show there were no hard feelings. She was content to leave Maggie's future in Angus's capable hands, knowing that with him as her husband Maggie would not be open to the same pressures from her brother.

By the time Natalie returned home she found that the happiness of her friend served to highlight the emptiness of her own life. For the first time she experienced a deep sense of self-pity which made her glad that from tomorrow she would be free to lead her own life again. But somehow the thought of spending her days with toddlers, even though she loved them, no longer seemed the right thing to do, and she wondered if it wouldn't be wiser to find a job which would bring her in touch with people of her own age. Old emotions were more easily forgotten if they were replaced by new ones, and it was this knowledge that prompted her to ring up an ex-boy-friend who was now director of an advertising agency, and ask if she could come and talk to him.

'By all means,' he said at once. 'I'm free tonight, if you are, and I've got tickets for the new show at the Royal. We can talk afterwards over dinner.'

It was churlish to refuse. Besides, an active social life was part of the cure she was planning for herself.

'I'd love to come,' she said.

'I'll collect you at seven. Dress up, angel, and we'll go dancing later.'

CHAPTER ELEVEN

WHEN she opened the door to David Sumner an hour later, the look Natalie saw on his face was ample compensation for the time she had taken with her appearance.

'No need to ask if you're well,' he said appreciatively. 'You look radiant!'

His eyes travelled slowly from the dark red cluster of curls which crowned her head, down the column of her slender throat, past tilted breasts to rest on a waist that was considerably smaller than when he had seen it last. 'You're thinner,' he added, 'but it suits you.'

'Thin enough to be a model?' she questioned.

'Don't tell me you're ready to give up potting toddlers!'

She laughed. 'I'm thinking of it. That's why I wanted to talk to you.'

'You aren't dumb enough to be a model.' He tucked his arm beneath hers and led her to a waiting taxi. 'I've a much better idea for you,' he continued. 'Why not take a job in my office? It would be much more in line with your brains—and your beauty won't come amiss there either.' He leaned forward and nibbled her ear. 'I'm glad you called me, Natalie, and I really could use you in the office. You're intelligent and educated, and six months from now you could be taking on your own accounts.'

'You really think so?'

'I'm sure of it. We'll talk about it during dinner.'

She nodded, and though she would have liked to continue with the discussion now, knew it would seem too pushy if she did. It was months since she had seen David and she thought him as good-looking now as when she had met him. But the spark had never been there, as far as she was concerned, and she had decided not to see him any more. Now she did not want him to get the wrong idea, and she pondered how to put this tactfully.

'I hope you'll like the play.' David's voice broke into her thoughts and she saw he was taking out some money to pay the taxi. 'Don't blame me if it's no good.'

'I'll bear that in mind before I run out on you,' she teased, and followed him into the auditorium.

It was crowded, and the majority of the audience were in evening dress. Photographers' flashbulbs popped as celebrities paused obligingly. Several people watched Natalie's progress into the stalls and with amusement she was aware of David's pride in her company.

'I bet every man in the theatre is envying me,' he whispered as they sat down. 'You're still the most stunning looking girl I know.'

'I bet you say that to all your girl-friends!'

'I wish I could,' he said ruefully, 'but it only applies to you.'

A flippant reply died in her throat as her gaze rested on the occupants of a box a few yards away. Even distance could not disguise Miles Denton's aristocratic features, nor hide the gleam in his eyes as they rested on her. She knew instinctively that he had watched her progress down to her seat, and she was delighted she was with such a personable escort.

Casually, as if she had not seen him, Natalie turned her attention to David, but was unable to see anything other than the memory of Miles and the honey-blonde girl beside him. Why should I be surprised because he's with Gayle? she thought angrily, but still found it impossible to focus on what David was saying.

'Don't you think so?' he queried with a smile.

'I do,' she nodded, and was relieved to find she had said the right thing.

At that moment the lights dimmed and the curtain parted, and Natalie let out a sigh and focused her eyes upon the stage.

For the first five minutes she was oblivious of what was happening there, but gradually she conquered her turmoil and was able to concentrate on the action taking place in front of her. She knew that in the interval David would expect her to make some intelligent comment, and resolutely she tried not to look up at the box where Miles was sitting. Yet from time to time she could not prevent herself. The sight of his clear-cut profile and the pale gleam of Gayle beside him hurt her more than she had believed possible.

They were with another couple, not Sir Elton and his wife, and she was relieved, for they might have spoken to her during the interval. But Gayle will keep a mile away from me, she thought ironically, and Miles will ignore me, so there's no need to sit trembling like an idiot!

When the curtain came down on the first act, she followed David to the bar, where he ordered champagne.

'There are some friends of mine over there,' he said, and waved his hand towards Imogen Houlder, a well-known actress, and her husband, who immediately came over to join them.

Natalie relaxed, glad to let the conversation carry on around her, and occasionally gave a smile to disguise the fact that her thoughts were miles away. Every fibre of her body seemed to be concentrated on the door, as if waiting for Miles to come through it, and when he at last appeared with Gayle clinging to his arm, she felt a stab of intense jealousy.

Feverishly she entered into the conversation, uttering a *bon mot* which made everyone laugh, and at least proving to herself that she was still capable of putting on an act that could fool anyone.

'Let's have dinner together afterwards,' Imogen Houlder suggested.

'Not tonight, angel.' David glanced from the actress to Natalie, and Imogen, seeing the look, gave him a knowing smile.

'No, dear,' David said, 'I'm not laying siege to Natalie, but we do have business to talk about.'

'Monkey business,' drawled the actress dryly. 'I refuse to believe you would ever talk business to a beautiful redhead after ten p.m.!'

Natalie smiled, but felt the curve of her lips stiffen as she saw Gayle come into view beyond Imogen's shoulder.

'Hello, Natalie,' the younger girl said in artless tones. 'It's ages since we met.'

Wishing it could have been longer, Natalie gave her a polite smile and hoped the girl would move on. But Gayle remained where she was, smiling first at Imogen and her husband and then at David. Natalie was obliged to introduce him to her, and Gayle spun out the pleasantries for so long that Miles, turning away from the bar with two drinks in his hand, was forced to bring them over.

As he approached, Natalie found her trembling ceased as though by magic, and from somewhere came a strength she had not thought she possessed. It enabled her to give him a cool smile and to speak to him in honeyed tones as she put her hand in David's and introduced the two men.

'Denton?' David repeated the name. 'You wouldn't be anything to do with Denton Engineering?'

'Jack Denton is my uncle,' Miles said, 'but I'm not in the same line of business.'

'Miles is a surgeon,' said Natalie. 'He cuts people up.'

'In my life,' David grinned, 'it's the women who do that!'

Miles gave a slight smile and handed Gayle her drink. Seen at close range, Natalie found, he was exactly as she had remembered him. Yet not quite the same, for though he had always been thin, he was now verging on the haggard. This in no way detracted from his looks; if anything it made him look more distinguished. His eyes glowed like amber coals and she could imagine how vivid they must appear when the rest of his face was covered by a surgical mask. She remembered the last time she had seen him glowing down at her and wondered if he ever remembered that moment when they had lain together on the settee and had so nearly allowed their mutual desire to reach fulfilment; might have done so too, if the telephone had not rung.

The glass in her hand trembled and some champagne spilled on her fingers.

'Here, let me take that,' David said, and did so, gently wiping her hand.

Natalie wondered why Gayle did not move away, but it seemed she had come for a purpose and was not to be dissuaded from it.

'I suppose you know of Miles's new appointment at the hospital?' she cooed.

'No one is interested in that,' Miles intervened, and put his hand on Gayle's arm as if to draw her away.

'I'd love to hear about your new appointment.' Natalie spoke directly to him, anxious to show that the anger with which she had faced him a month ago had been completely forgotten. 'I hadn't realised Sir Elton was retiring quite so soon,' she continued.

'He had a slight heart attack,' Miles told her, his eyes still impersonal as they met hers. 'That somewhat precipitated things.'

'So now you've reached the top of the ladder?'

'The youngest surgeon ever to hold such a position,' Gayle trilled, and leaned close to Miles, her long blonde hair brushing his chin as she clung to his arm. 'But he hates it when I tell everyone.'

'It's a job like any other,' he shrugged.

'But you're brilliant at it, darling,' Gayle pouted. 'Why shouldn't I be proud of you?'

Miles shrugged and spoke to David. 'You mentioned my uncle. Do you know him?'

'Very well. My company handles his advertising.'

'Now *you're* in a tough business,' Miles smiled. 'Pretty cut-throat, too, I should imagine.'

'That's what Natalie used to say. Though now she's jumping on to the band wagon, I'm glad to say.'

Natalie wished she had warned David not to mention her plans, but it was too late, for Miles was looking at her with an enigmatic smile.

'So you're renouncing the toddlers for something more lucrative? You always gave me the impression that you cared about them.'

'I still do. But I also care about enjoying my own life,' she said. 'I've been looking after children for five years and I need a break.'

'She can always return to it when she gets married,' David put in, and slipped his arm around her waist.

Natalie leaned against him. 'You never know,' she smiled, and though she despised herself for flirting, she was determined to show Miles she was heart whole.

'Can we go back to our seats now, darling?' Gayle asked Miles, as if she had said all she wished to say.

He nodded to Natalie and David, smiled at their friends, and led Gayle away.

'A good-looking couple,' Imogen commented, her eyes on the man. 'And definitely the marrying kind.'

'Doctors have to be,' her husband replied. 'It makes their women patients feel safe with them.'

'I wouldn't want to feel safe with Mr Denton!'

'You would, if he had you on an operating table.'

'That isn't where I was thinking of him putting me!' Imogen's warm glance at her husband made it clear she was joking, and his returning glance showed that he knew it.

David smiled at Natalie. 'You seemed to know Denton. Is he a friend of yours?'

'I went out with him a couple of times, but I wouldn't call him a friend.'

'Good.'

The theatre bell rang and they returned to their seats. It required all Natalie's strength of mind for her to pay attention to the play, and she was relieved when the curtain finally came down.

In the foyer she again came face to face with Gayle, who was waiting while Miles went to get the car.

'You wait here too, darling,' said David. 'It's raining hard and it may take me a while to get a cab.'

To remain alone with Gayle was the last thing Natalie wanted, but David disappeared in the crush before she could follow him, and Gayle edged closer and successfully stuck at her elbow.

'Miles looks tired, don't you think?' she murmured.

'I didn't look at him closely enough to notice,' Natalie replied indifferently.

'He's working terribly hard,' Gayle went on, 'and we're house-hunting too. Miles and I both think his house in Harley Street is too inconvenient to be made into a proper home. Anyway, I'd hate to live in a medical atmosphere.'

Natalie's tongue was dry and she could not twist it into any words, but Gayle did not seem to notice the silence and went on chatting.

'When I say we're house-hunting, I really mean *I* am. Miles is leaving it mainly to me. After all, I'm the one who'll be there most of the time.' The artless voice stopped momentarily before continuing. 'I did tell you we're getting married, didn't I?'

'I assumed you wouldn't be living in sin!' Natalie was pleased she could finally manage to speak, and in the noise and rush around them she hoped the shakiness of her voice was not apparent.

'Miles wants us to keep it quiet until the excitement of his new appointment has died down,' Gayle added. 'Otherwise people might think he married me because of who Daddy is.'

'Surely no one could think such an obvious thing,' Natalie said smoothly, and was pleased to see the colour come up and go in the pale skin in front of her.

But Gayle was too clever to rise to the jibe and she turned her head as though looking for Miles. Then muttering: 'I think I can see him,' she weaved her way through the crowds.

Natalie waited for several moments before following, giving Miles time to pull away before going outside. She immediately saw David's wild gesticulations from the window of a cab, and she ran towards it and jumped in. She longed to tell him to take her home, but decided it would be easier to face him across a table and huddled back in a corner of the taxi. She was shivering though she was not cold, and knew her trembling came from nerves. She wanted to burst into tears. How could Miles be foolish enough to marry Gayle? Even if he had decided that loving herself was wrong for him, he surely couldn't believe that loving Gayle was right?

'You haven't forgotten you're taking me dancing,' she said to David, in an artificially gay voice.

'I've been thinking of it all evening. It's the only way I ever get to hold you.' He caught her hand. 'It'll be wonderful to have you working with me.'

'I haven't made a decision yet,' she warned. 'I want to think about it.'

'You'll forgive me if I try to be a little more persuasive before the evening ends?'

'Don't be too persuasive or you'll frighten me off!'

Taking the hint, David behaved in an exemplary fashion for the rest of the evening; flirting with her, yet remaining casual, as if he knew that now was not the time for anything more.

'I hope you'll decide to join me at the agency,' he said when he left her outside her front door. 'It will do you good to change jobs, Natalie.'

Promising to think carefully before making up her mind, Natalie left him and prepared for bed. Much as she wanted to find work that would occupy her mind, she knew that working for David might create more problems than it solved, and that it would be better to work with people who did not know her.

Yet wherever she worked she was bound to meet men who would want to take her out. That was part of the penalty of looking the way she did. Yet it had far too many compensations for her to regret it. The truth was that there was only one man whom she wanted, and seeing him again had made that all too clear.

CHAPTER TWELVE

A FEW days later Natalie dropped David a note to say she had decided against leaving the nursery school. As she had expected, she received an irate telephone call from him, demanding to know why she had made such a foolish decision. But she would not allow herself to be dissuaded from it.

'All right,' he said finally, 'so stay with the tots. But that doesn't mean you have to drop out of my life. I'm still crazy about you, Natalie.'

'That was why I stopped seeing you last time,' she reminded him. 'I don't want you to be hurt.'

'I'm a big boy and I can take care of myself.'

'I'll call you,' she promised, knowing she would do no such thing, and hung up before he had a chance to remonstrate with her.

Time passed slowly. It was now a month since she had seen Miles at the theatre, but she still kept re-living every word of her last scene with Gayle. It was so vivid that everything the girl had said was etched on her mind. She wished Gayle had also told her when the wedding would be. Knowing the worst might help her to face up to the fact that Miles had completely gone from her life.

It was incredible that he had come to mean so much to her in so short a time. Why should one feel so strongly attracted towards one human being and not to another? After all, from a logical point of view David was as eligible as Miles. He was better-looking too, and would certainly be a far easier husband, since he was amusing, undemanding, and would have much more time to devote to her.

Miles, on the other hand, was undoubtedly quick-tempered, and he worked long and erratic hours that would inevitably affect his social life. Yet how happily she would have married him, knowing all this. Married him and loved him for the rest of her life.

But the rest of her life had to be lived without him, and though at the moment she could not consider putting any other man in his place, she knew that her natural resilience would one day make this possible. But not yet. First she had to cope with the problem of day-to-day living and tell herself that the pain she felt today would lessen and eventually disappear.

Yet the shadows of sleeplessness lay like bruises beneath her eyes and her slenderness increased—a fact which both Maggie and Angus commented on when she attended their wedding.

She had deliberately seen less of Maggie since her friend had returned from Scotland, knowing she was busy selling her business as well as looking for a flat for herself and Angus.

Over and above these reasons, she did not want to bump into Roland who, as far as she could gather from Maggie's last telephone call to her, was still seeing Gillian. It seemed as if Miles was unable—or was no longer concerned—to prevent his sister from continuing to make a fool of herself. Natalie wondered cynically if he had decided he was being presumptuous in trying to control the lives of other people, no matter how dear they were to him.

Roland himself supplied the answer to this when Natalie saw him at Maggie's wedding. All of Angus's family had come down from Scotland for the event, and there was a large crowd of people both in the church and at the reception, which was held in a small but extremely pleasant Bayswater hotel.

Maggie was radiant with happiness, and though even as a bride she could not have been called beautiful, it was easy to see from Angus's adoring eyes that to him she epitomised everything he wanted in a wife.

'You must get married next,' said Maggie, coming over to make sure Natalie was enjoying herself.

'Wait until you're an old married woman before you start matchmaking,' Natalie warned.

'It's just that I'm so happy, I want you to be happy too.'

'Why assume one can only be happy in the married state? Don't you know how old-fashioned that idea is?'

'It may be old-fashioned for some people, but not for us.' Maggie lowered her voice. 'Did you know Roland isn't seeing Gillian Denton any more?'

'No.' Natalie's heart thumped heavily in her chest. 'What happened?'

'I don't know. All Roland says is that he got bored with her.'

'I don't believe your brother would ever get bored with a rich girl,' Natalie said frankly. 'She must have given him the push.'

Maggie sighed and then smiled, refusing to let her worries about Roland mar this particular day. 'He may be going to Canada,' she continued. 'He's been offered a job there.'

'The further from you the better,' Natalie replied. 'You know what I think of him.'

'Only too well,' Maggie smiled, and turned to talk to some of her other guests.

Not for a moment did Natalie believe Roland's story, and she would have dearly liked to know what had finally made Gillian decide to break with him. Or had propinquity done the trick where threats and pressure had failed?

She looked up as someone slid into the chair next to her, and saw with dismay that it was Roland.

'I know how delighted you are to see me,' he drawled, 'so don't bother to widen your smile.'

'As a matter of fact I was thinking about you,' she said with honesty. 'I hear you're not seeing Gillian Denton.'

'Has that made you happy?'

'I'm happy for any girl who comes to her senses where you're concerned.'

'Still my devoted admirer, I see!'

'When are you going to Canada?'

Roland laughed and Natalie, hearing herself put the question, had to laugh too.

'Yes,' she admitted, 'I can't wait for you to get out of Maggie's hair. Not that you'll find her such an easy touch now she's married to Angus.'

'I know,' he said ruefully. 'I haven't lost a little sister, but I've gained a big brother!' He glanced at his smooth hands. 'I'll be leaving England in a fortnight and, if I don't like Canada, I'll go on to the States.'

'What happened between you and Gillian?' Natalie asked, and regretted the impulsiveness which had made her ask the question, for she knew Roland would not be able to resist trying to hurt her with his reply.

'It was a mutual parting of the ways,' he said. 'I'm sorry it came too late to prevent your break-up with the wonderful surgeon, but I hope it's taught you not to interfere in other people's affairs.'

'I'll always enjoy interferring in *your* affairs, Roland —if only to save a female from ruining her life.' Natalie kept a cool smile on her face and resisted the urge to lift her handbag and bring it down upon his head. 'I suppose Gillian finally realised what a swine you were. Or did a richer bird come your way?'

'I'll leave you to guess the answer. I wouldn't want to prevent your fertile little imagination from working overtime.' He moved away and then stopped and looked at her over his shoulder. 'Of course you could ring up the surgeon and ask him. I'm sure he'd love to tell you.'

Natalie watched Roland disappear behind a group of people, and wished bitterly that he had never come into her life. At least she would not have met Miles. She glanced at her watch, but knew she could not leave the reception until Angus and Maggie had left for their honeymoon. This meant at least another hour of false gaiety for her.

Draining her glass of champagne, she went over to the bar to get another one. Too much of it would give her a headache, but at least it would blot out the misery which pervaded her.

'Natalie!' Her name was called and she saw Maggie waving to her. 'Angus and I are leaving in a moment,' her friend whispered as she reached her side. 'But we want to go off as quietly as we can, otherwise we'll get showered with confetti and rice.'

'I don't see how you can avoid it.'

'We've got it all worked out,' said Maggie. 'I'll leave the room with you and everyone will think we're going off to have a last girlish gossip. Then a few minutes later Angus will slip out and meet me at the side entrance of the hotel. That's where he's parked his car.'

'With all the old boots tied to it!' Natalie chuckled.

'Angus collected his new car yesterday,' Maggie said proudly, 'so no one even knows which one is his.'

'What a cunning, well matched couple you are. I bet you met through the Whitney Marriage Bureau!'

Laughing together, the girls linked arms and walked out of the room. Once in the corridor, they made their way smartly down the stairs to the lobby.

'I saw you talking to my in-laws,' said Maggie, still moving quickly. 'They're nice, aren't they?'

'Very. They asked me to have dinner with them this evening.'

'You didn't say you would?' Maggie asked instantly.

'No, I didn't. But I'm beginning to regret it. I have nothing else fixed and I don't fancy going home alone.'

'I'm sure you won't do that.'

They reached the rear entrance of the hotel and Maggie paused. 'We might as well wait here for a minute,' she said. 'Angus won't have left the reception yet.'

'Do you want me to wait with you,' Natalie asked, 'or shall I go back?'

'Certainly not!' Maggie caught her arm in a vicelike grip. 'Stay and talk to me until Angus comes.'

Natalie did so for some five minutes before Angus's tall figure loomed over them.

'No one suspects a thing,' he said truthfully. 'They think I've gone off in search of you, and they are all massing in the foyer for the big send-off.'

'I'm beginning to feel sorry for everybody.' Maggie's laughing voice belied her words and she caught Angus by the hand as they went out to the street. Cars were ranged along one side of the road, bumper to bonnet, and Angus stopped by a bright blue saloon.

'A bit different from my old jalopy,' he said proudly.

'Are you talking about your new wife?' Natalie questioned, and Angus laughed and swung round to give her a hug.

'I'll never forget what you did for Maggie when she was ill,' he said, 'and I hope you'll look on me as a friend too.'

'I do already,' she said warmly, and hugged him back, then blinked away her tears as she kissed Maggie and helped her to get into the car.

Angus seemed to be taking an inordinately long time to put the key into the ignition, and Natalie looked anxiously back at the hotel. 'Do hurry up and go before someone comes round from the front and sees you.'

'We'll be away soon,' he muttered, taking the key out again and looking at it. 'This can't be the right one,' he frowned, and searched among the bunch for another.

Natalie looked at Maggie, who smiled back at her, not seeming at all put out by her husband's inability to start the car. Once again Angus went to switch on the ignition and once again the engine failed to start.

'I suppose this *is* your car?' Natalie asked, bending down to speak to him through the window.

'Of course it is.' The corners of his mouth were twitching slightly. Obviously he thought it funny that they were unable to go, especially after the efforts they had made to thwart their friends.

Unexpectedly Maggie gave him a sharp nudge and he suddenly seemed to find the right key and put it into the lock. The engine raced and Angus slowly edged the car out.

Maggie blew Natalie a kiss. ''Bye, darling. Have a lovely evening!'

'And you,' Natalie called, then giggled and went on

waving until the car swung further out and moved nippily away.

For a long moment Natalie remained where she was. Then with a heavy sigh she turned back to the pavement. Her body came up against a hard unyielding force and with a murmur of apology she looked up. The strength seemed to drain from her as she stared into Miles's clear cut face.

'Goodness!' she said abruptly. 'We always seem to be bumping into each other.'

'It wasn't an accident this time.' He cleared his throat. 'I—er—I'm afraid I was late.'

'Late?' she repeated uncomprehendingly.

'I couldn't find a parking spot nearby, and I was still at the top of the road when I saw Angus climbing into his car.' A half smile played round the corners of his mouth as he saw her looking at him as if he had gone out of his mind. 'I'm trying to explain why Angus was so dense about getting his car started,' Miles said. 'He was giving me time to catch up with you.'

'You mean he—you mean he knew you were coming here?'

'They both did.'

Natalie was stunned; but only momentarily. 'Then you could all have saved yourself the effort. I have nothing to say to you.'

Summarily she turned and began to walk away from Miles. But her intention was foiled by his adroitly sidestepping and blocking her way.

'I want to talk to you first, Natalie. If you want to leave after you've heard me, I won't stop you.'

His implacable expression warned her she would not be able to push past him, and she gave a nod.

'We can't talk here,' he continued, and gripping her

firmly round the waist, marched her to where his car was parked. Quickly he opened the door and pushed her down into the passenger seat, then rapidly moved round the car and seated himself next to her.

'I don't grovel very well,' he said abruptly, 'but if it will help you to forgive me, I'll do it willingly.'

'I suppose you're referring to Gillian and Roland?'

'What else? It's the only thing we quarrelled about.'

'Not quite,' Natalie said carefully. 'Our quarrel was concerned with other things too.'

'What other things?'

'Your basic distrust of women. Your fear of marriage. Those were the things that made you doubt me.'

'Rubbish!'

'Those were the reasons why you asked me to pretend to be your girl-friend,' she persisted. 'If you hadn't been scared of getting married, Gayle would have hooked you years ago.'

'Did it never strike you that I remained unhooked— as you so charmingly put it—because I wasn't in love with Gayle?'

'Is that why you're going to marry her now?' Furiously Natalie turned her back on him and stared out of the side window. 'If you want to appease your conscience by apologising for what you said, take it as done. But please don't make me stay here and listen to anything more. I'm not in the mood.'

There was silence.

'Because I'm going to marry Gayle?' he asked finally.

'You're intelligent enough to do what's best for you,' she said coldly.

'Which is why I'm here,' he replied, and Natalie felt him move along the seat until his voice was close in her ear. 'I probably deserve to marry a tough little nut like

Gayle, but luckily we don't always get what we deserve. If we did, I wouldn't have a hope in hell of getting you.'

'Don't worry about it,' she snapped, 'you won't!'

'Won't I?' So quickly that she was taken by surprise, his arms came around her and his hands were hard against her waist. 'I love you, Natalie, and I'm going to make you believe me if I have to spend the whole weekend repeating it.'

His closeness made her tremble, but it did not lessen the bitterness she felt at the way he had misjudged her.

'There's no love without trust, Miles, and you made your lack of trust all too clear.'

'I know,' he said huskily. 'I hated myself for it almost as soon as I'd said it. I wanted to tell you weeks ago that I loved you, but I couldn't find the courage. Then by the time I made up my mind to come round to your flat, it was too late.'

'Too late?' she asked in a stilted voice.

'I saw you at the theatre. You looked so radiantly beautiful and happy that I—that it seemed I mean nothing to you.'

She drew a deep shuddering breath, astonished he could have thought she looked happy when she had been crying out with longing for him.

'If you judge your patients' conditions as cleverly,' she snapped, 'you probably kill more than you cure!'

'I'm not blinded by love when I deal with my patients,' he said roughly, and pulled her round to face him.

A patch of red stained either cheek, giving him unusual colour and telling her more clearly than anything he could have said what a heightened state of tension he was in. Gone was the cool surgeon who was always in command of himself. Here was a man torn apart by the need to make amends and not caring how deeply he had to abject himself in order to do it.

'When I accused you of finding women for Roland, I knew I was talking like a madman. But I was in such a flaming temper with you that I didn't care what I said. By the time I got home that night I already regretted it, but I was afraid to come back and tell you in case you threw me out again.'

'Which I would have done.'

'That's why I left it,' he repeated. 'And the longer I stayed away the more scared I became to go back to see you.'

This was so unlike the positive man she believed him to be that Natalie found it hard to accept he was speaking the truth. Her look gave away her thoughts and Miles sighed deeply and rubbed one hand across his forehead.

'See it from my point of view, Natalie,' he murmured. 'You're beautiful and full of life—far too beautiful to want to tie yourself to a dull stick like me. I even told myself that marriage to me would ruin your life and that you deserved someone better, someone who could give you an active social life where you can shine. All I can give you is an overworked man with a tetchy disposition.'

'Don't underestimate yourself,' she cried vehemently, and put her hands on either side of his face. 'I don't want an active social life where I can shine. I want you, you stupid, stupid thing!'

'I am a stupid thing,' he agreed, and gathered her close.

He was trembling as violently as she was, and seemed content merely to hold her against him and breathe in the scent of her.

'You're right about my being scared of women,' he confessed softly. 'I've always found them difficult to talk to and impossible to understand. Gayle was the only one with whom I felt at ease—which is why I let her become so involved in my life.'

Natalie snuggled into his shoulder. 'It's a good thing I came along and saved you. Otherwise you might have ended up marrying her.'

'That stupid I'm not,' he said with conviction. 'But it would have meant a pretty painful row. Instead of which I evolved the brilliant scheme of using you, which killed one bird and found me another. You see, I knew from the first moment I met you that I wasn't going to let you walk out of my life.'

'I don't believe that,' she said, tilting her head to look at him.

'It's true, my darling. The moment you started yelling back at me, with your eyes sparkling with fury, I knew I'd found the woman for me.' His lips moved down and rested against the side of her mouth. 'Why else do you think I took you home to meet my mother so quickly? I was scared of losing you. I just used Gayle as an excuse.'

'Yet you still doubted me over Roland.' Even now Natalie did not find it easy to forgive him.

'You have every right to be bitter,' he said gravely. 'The only way I can promise it won't occur again is for you to live with me and help me to understand myself more.'

With a murmur she relaxed completely against him, and he kissed her deeply, as if wanting to draw the sweetness of her into himself.

'Let's go back to my house,' he said huskily.

She nodded and he moved back and set the car in

motion. Miles drove fast, not speaking but occasionally half turning to give her a smile that set her heart pounding. Finally he drew up in Harley Street and led her up the steps of his house.

His hands were jerky as he unlocked the front door and pulled her into the hall. Only then did he come to a full stop, staring at her with a blank intensity that made her feel he was not seeing her at all.

'What's wrong, Miles? Why are you looking at me so oddly?'

'Because I——' He stopped and moistened his lips. 'Because holding you back there in the car made me realise what my life would be like if you didn't forgive me. That's why I've brought you here. I had to get you alone; I had to convince you how much you mean to me.'

Blindly he reached out for her. His body was shuddering and he pushed her back against the wall and pressed himself upon her, his thighs heaving against her own.

'I love you, Natalie, I love you,' he said over and over again. 'And I'm never going to let you go.'

He gave her no chance to reply, kissing her with a ferocity he had never shown before. She felt the fierce pressure of his fingers as they dug into her shoulders and instinctively she knew that to fight him would be dangerous. Instead she forced herself to go limp and sagged against him like a rag doll. For a few seconds he went on pressing kisses along the side of her throat. Then he became aware of the weight of her, and with an incoherent exclamation he swung her up into his arms.

'Darling, forgive me! I didn't mean to hurt you.'

Effortlessly he carried her across the hall to his consulting room. He kicked open the door and strode across to place her carefully down on the examination couch. Only as he went to step back did she reach out and catch his hand.

'I'm all right, Miles,' she said softly. 'It's just that you—that you frightened me.'

'I was beginning to frighten myself.' Soberly he leaned over and regarded her. 'Lie still and I'll get you something to take.'

'I don't need anything.' She still kept hold of his hand. 'Tell me what happened between Gillian and Roland.'

'Must we talk about them now?'

'Yes, please. Then we need never talk about Roland again.'

'Great!' His look was wry. 'Gillian finally came to her senses. I made it clear that if she married him she wouldn't get a penny from her Trust. She said she didn't believe me, but to her credit she apparently had enough sense to make Roland believe that I meant it. The rest you can work out for yourself.'

'His love disappeared and Canada beckoned.'

Miles nodded. 'At least one of the Dentons showed some intelligence. When I remember the things I said to you....'

'Stop remembering,' she chided. 'Think of the future instead.'

'*Our* future,' he said, lowering his head to rest his mouth on hers. 'I hope you don't want a long engagement?'

'Three months,' she whispered, gazing into his eyes.

'Make it three weeks, then Angus and Maggie will be back.'

'What made you come to their wedding?' Natalie asked. 'I didn't even know you knew them.'

'I was called in to see a patient in Angus's hospital and he was the doctor in charge. We had to speak together privately, and he took the opportunity to call me a coward for not having the courage to apologise to you. When a junior doctor talks to you in that way, you know he feels pretty deeply about it.'

Darling Angus, Natalie thought, and her eyes filled with tears of joy. Seeing them, Miles wrapped his arms around her and lowered himself upon the couch until he rested his head upon her breasts.

'It's a good thing the Medical Council can't see me now,' he whispered. 'This is definitely not what a doctor's couch is for!'

'But I'm not the doctor's patient,' she murmured.

'Nor are you the doctor's wife,' he replied. 'Though if you go on looking at me so enticingly, you could well become one before the legal knot is tied.'

Memory of something Gayle had said made Natalie push him slightly away. 'Gayle told me you were looking for another house to live in.'

'I am,' he said. 'But I'll gladly stay here if you would prefer it.'

'I'll do whatever you wish. All that matters is that we're together.'

He gave her a lopsided smile, looking so boyish that she felt her heart turn over in her breast. 'But if we remain here,' she said, 'I'd like to change the decor upstairs.'

'Let's go and have a look at it,' he replied, pulling her to her feet and leading her slowly to the lift.

In the small space they clung together unashamedly as they rose slowly to the top floor. It was taking them heavenwards, thought Natalie, and knew that wherever Miles was, that was where her heaven would always be.

The Mills & Boon Rose is the Rose of Romance

Every month there are ten new titles to choose from — ten new stories about people falling in love, people you want to read about, people in exciting, far-away places. Choose Mills & Boon. It's your way of relaxing.

May's titles are:

PAGAN LOVER *by Anne Hampson*
Tara had been forced to marry the masterful Leon Petrides and there was no escape — but did she really want to get away?

GARDEN OF THORNS *by Sally Wentworth*
Somebody was trying to get rid of Kirsty, but she just *couldn't* believe it was the autocratic Squire, Gyles Grantham.

KELLY'S MAN *by Rosemary Carter*
Kelly found it very galling that, despite all her efforts, Nicholas Van Mijden should still persist in thinking of her as just a spoiled rich girl.

DEBT OF DISHONOUR *by Mary Wibberley*
Renata's job was to look after a difficult teenage girl — but she found the girl's forbidding uncle more difficult and unpredictable to deal with!

CRESCENDO *by Charlotte Lamb*
'If you let them, women will take you over completely,' was Gideon Firth's philosophy — and that philosophy had ruined Marina's life.

BAY OF STARS *by Robyn Donald*
Bourne Kerwood had been described as 'a handsome bundle of dynamite' — and that dynamite had exploded all over Lorena's young life!

DARK ENCOUNTER *by Susanna Firth*
'For the salary you're offering I'd work for the devil himself' — and when Kate started work for Nicholas Blake she soon began to wonder if that wasn't just what she *was* doing...

MARRIAGE BY CAPTURE *by Margaret Rome*
Married against her will, Claire promised herself that the marriage would be in name only — but that promise was a surprisingly difficult one to keep!

BINDABURRA OUTSTATION *by Kerry Allyne*
'Go back to the city where you belong,' ordered Kelly Sinclair contemptuously, and Paige would have been only too glad to oblige — but fate forestalled her...

APOLLO'S DAUGHTER *by Rebecca Stratton*
Bethany resented Nikolas Meandis when he tried to order her life for her — and that was before she realised just what he was planning for her...!

If you have difficulty in obtaining any of these books from your local paperback retailer, write to:
Mills & Boon Reader Service
P.O. Box 236, Thornton Road, Croydon, Surrey CR9 3RU.

Just what the Doctor ordered!

Don't miss the two Doctor-Nurse Romances published every month.

These titles highlight the romantic entanglements between doctors, nurses surgeons and sisters who are involved every day with life and death decisions. Surrounded as they are by constant pressure and emotion, it is no wonder that passions run high behind the scenes of modern hospital life.

Available where you buy paperbacks. If you have difficulty in obtaining these at your normal retailer, contact Mills & Boon Reader Service, P.O. Box 236, Thornton Road, Croydon, CR9 3RU

Masquerade

Intrigue excitement romance...

Masquerade is an enthralling series of Historical Romances. As you read you will be transported back to an age of true romance... to the courts of eleventh-century Spain... to Regency England. From secret assignations in secluded country lanes to high intrigue in glittering chandelier-lit ballrooms.

You will lose yourself in a world where the smile of a beautiful woman could change the course of history.

Every month Masquerade offers you two new romances set against authentic historical backgrounds. You'll find them where paperbacks are sold.

Mills & Boon Classics

~all that's best in romantic fiction

The very greatest of
Mills & Boon romances brought back
for those who never had the
opportunity of reading them
on the first time of publication.
Collect these stories of love
and romance set in exotic,
faraway places and fill your library
with Mills & Boon Classics.

Available where you buy paperbacks.

If you have difficulty
in obtaining these at your
normal retailer, contact
Mills & Boon Reader Service,
P.O. Box 236, Thornton Road,
Croydon, CR9 3RU.